# Blurred

# Blurred

## Iris Wolff

Translated by Ruth Martin
Edited by Monique Charlesworth

First published in German as
Die Unschärfe der Welt by Klett-Cotta in 2020

Moth Books Ltd, PO BOX 80244, London W9 4LN

Published in English by Moth Books 2025

Copyright © 2020 Klett-Cotta – J.G. Cotta' sche Buchhandlung Nachfolger GmbH, Stuttgart/Germany

This edition published by arrangement with
Gaeb & Eggers Literary Agency

English Translation © Ruth Martin 2024

The moral rights of the author and translator have been asserted

All rights reserved. No part of this publication may be reproduced, stored in a retrieval system or transmitted in any form or by any means, electronic, mechanical, photocopying, recording or otherwise, without prior written permission of the author.

Manufacturer: York Publishing Services Ltd
64 Hallfield Road, Layerthorpe, York YO31 7ZQ
Tel: 01904 431213 | Email: enquiries@yps-publishing.co.uk
Website: www.yps-publishing.co.uk

Represented by: Authorised Rep Compliance Ltd.
Ground Floor, 71 Lower Baggot Street, Dublin D02 P593, Ireland
www.arccompliance.com

ISBN 978-1-917593-00-7
ISBN 978-1-917593-01-4 (ebook)

Edited by Monique Charlesworth
Typeset by Clare Brayshaw
Cover design by Dan Jones

The translation of this book was supported by a grant
from the Goethe-Institut

*For Andreas*

*I saw
the stone melt
and the love go,*

*the bird called out
from the tree.*

*We say:
He's singing*

Richard Wagner

# AWARDS

*Blurred* was nominated for the German Book Prize, the Bavarian Book Prize (Fiction) and the Wilhelm Raabe Literature Prize in 2020; in 2021 *Blurred* won the Evangelical Book Prize and the LiteraTour North Prize. The same year, Iris Wolff was presented with three literary awards: the Solothurn Literature Prize, the Eichendorff Literary Prize and the Marie Luise-Kaschnitz Prize.

'Iris Wolff tells the moving story of a family from the Banat so closely connected that even across borders these ties remain. Four generations tell of losses and new beginnings in a captivating style ... *Blurred* explores the lives of seven people, a family of choice who despite the blows of fate and the distances between them refuse to be separated. Against the background of the collapse of the Eastern Bloc and the eventful history of the 20th century, a great novel is born – about friendship and what we are prepared to give up to secure another person's happiness. With artistry and great precision, Iris Wolff explores the possibilities and the limitations of language and memory - and of the images others create in their own minds about who we really are.'

*Jury nomination, German Book Prize 2020*

## PRAISE FOR BLURRED

'Iris Wolff is a great storyteller ... This author uses language that is sensual and alive, while also understanding how to depict character both vividly and subtly. In the final pages, Iris Wolff ties together the artfully laid out threads connecting Stuttgart, Munich, Sylt and the Banat in a virtuoso manner. This is great, great storytelling.'

Günter Kaindlstorfer, *Deutschland radio*

'*Blurred* is an eminently poetic novel, employing the entire range of sensory and intellectual experiences and permeated by a political and historical reality. When you also take into account the extremely original narrative style, you can barely believe how easy this short novel is to read, or how entirely it succeeds.'

Pascal Mathéus, *Literaturkritik.de*

'Iris Wolff tells her story from a place of deep calm. She widens time. She gives us one century and several human lives in less than two hundred pages. Yet everything is there.'

Carsten Hueck, *SWR2 archive radio*

'An author with a dreamlike feel for language'

Denis Scheck, *Druckfrisch*

'No one else has made history float as beautifully as this'
Stefan Kister, *Stuttgarter Zeitung*

'Quietly, unobtrusively and vividly told, each individual in this ensemble of characters is portrayed by Wolff with compassion yet in so few words. A novel that continues to resonate. *Blurred* is quiet, reserved and yet highly intensive and extensive ... Iris Wolff is so embedded in the minds of nearly all her characters that they swiftly become memorable.'
Gerrit Bartels, *Tagesspiegel*

'A novel that is very diverse, poetic, political, psychologically astute and joyful'
Ann-Dore Krohn, *Literary Colloquium Berlin*

'To journey with her, to get involved in this novel and its wonderful prose, to immerse yourself in it – what a great and very touching experience.'
Denis Scheck, *Das Erste druckfrisch*

'This could be Iris Wolff's year. The novel ... tells a big story in a short space. The Banat setting will come as no surprise to readers familiar with Iris Wolff's previous books, all set in the formerly German-populated regions of Romania, in Transylvania or the Banat. Iris Wolff spent the first eight years of her life in these regions before her family emigrated to Germany in 1985; these unforgettable impressions of country and small-town life, a life seemingly out of time, are the source material for her novels; and for moments time itself is repeatedly brought to a stand-still in episodes of the highest literary intensity.

'"A story can be told so often and so vividly that you think you remember it yourself." This is precisely what comes to pass in *Blurred*. The last chapter, Prestigio, is named for the crescendo of a magic show. A perfect fit.'

Andreas Platthaus, *Frankfurter Allgemeine Zeitung*

'A hauntingly delicate narrative in language which creates the lightest of atmospheres, always with a faint undertone of melancholy.'

Pasc Eisenack, *Nürnberger Zeitung*

'Ultimately everything comes together to make a completely wonderful book, a magnficent and notably idiosyncratic novel, its sharply drawn characters arrayed on the horizon of twentieth century European history, on history bedded in the nostalgically beautiful landscape of the Banat ... A powerful story, a polyphonic concert.'

Wolfgang Wiedenhöfer, *Frisch vom Stapel*

'Her novel flows forth like a wide river, without making things easy for the reader. Those who let themselves be immersed will however be drawn into a mysterious world.'

Antje Scherer, *Märkische Oderzeitung*

'Iris Wolff's quiet narrative flow enchants. But it doesn't numb the reader, quite the reverse. You become more awake and more curious. The world of this novel is fully revealed in the language of an author who finely weaves thematic threads and connections through the whole text'

Carsten Hueck, *Ex Libris*

'Beautiful, clear images, uniting tough and gentle, depict lives shaped by political upheavals, personal tragedies and misdeeds, by individual courage, self-will, a hunger for life and a deep attachment to the soil'

Franziska Hirsbrunner, *Swiss Radio and Television SRF*

'One life touches another. People lose and then suddenly find one another again in childhood's landscapes of the soul. As if a magician was holding the loose threads of lives in her hand.'

Günter Ott, *Augsburger Allgemeine*

'Her novel ... insists on exact feelings and on seeing sharply – and it's precisely its lyrical tone that refuses to resolve contradictions'

Annette Hoffmann, *Badische Zeitung*

'Iris Wolff has written a wonderful, enchanting book'

Karin Servatius-Speck, *Siebenbürgische Zeitung*

'Here, strong characters move on quiet feet; suffering and blows of fate are seen as passing phenomena rather than focal points, and the tension places the accents where you least expect them ... Wolff's literature is poetic, rather than constructive; life itself does not follow dramaturgy.'

Irina Kilimnik, *Die Presse*

'The great quality she possesses is perhaps what Peter Handke (referring to Hermann Lenz) once called poetic history lessons. She has found a language ... that permits figures to appear, letting us see them through what they must endure. Iris Wolff has written another great novel.'

Rainer Moritz, *Norddeutscher Radio*

'Perhaps the great art of the storyteller Iris Wolff – who like that magician from Transylvania ended up in Stuttgart at a young age – is that through language alone, she transports us into a realm that lies beyond words. There is no escaping this magic.'

Stefan Kister, *Stuttgarter Zeitung*

'Iris Wolff has at her disposal an incredibly sophisticated psychological tool – an instrument she uses to draw her figures. It feels like watercolour, but afterwards you really feel wow – what a huge landscape has been drawn here.'

Denis Scheck, *WDR Westdeutscher Radio*

'A stroke of luck for German language literature'

Gérard Otremba, *Sounds and Books*

'Iris Wolff travels along the edges of political systems and transcends them … The author tells her story in a touching and a stirring manner; because the real background is often blurred, her characters and their experiences are tremendously vivid … There are unexpected reunions, some too lovely to be real, but the novel has a truth of its own. How good that it has been nominated for the German Book Prize.'

Cornelia Geißler, *Berliner Zeitung*

# CONTENTS

• • • • •

| | |
|---|---|
| Letter to readers in English from Iris Wolff | |
| Zăpadă | 1 |
| Echo | 29 |
| Leviathan | 55 |
| Wind wanderer | 77 |
| Macromolecular | 99 |
| Jupiter | 127 |
| Prestigio | 153 |
| | |
| Thanks and acknowledgements | 183 |
| Translator's note | 185 |
| Glossary of place names | 187 |

Dear readers,

When I begin a new novel, I don't know much about the world I am describing. I start with an image and that leads me into the story. I might have to wait a long time before this door opens; it has to come with a specific gut feeling which will show me that, of all possible stories, this is the one I want to tell. With *Blurred*, it was the image of Florentine riding through the snow on a horse-drawn sled. She is heavily pregnant and afraid for her child. Then the child, Samuel, is born – and this novel tells his story.

As my writing followed Florentine, she led me to the village where I grew up. A village of 6000 people in the Banat, a historical region that now lies in Romania. This village, like the rest of Eastern Europe, was home to various nationalities and languages: Slovakians, Serbs, Romanians, Hungarians, Romani and a German minority. My father was a Protestant pastor there, and my mother a nursery school teacher. I spent the first eight years of my life in the village, and with my grandparents in Hermannstadt (Sibiu).

My childhood home wrote itself into this novel: the house with its long hallway, the garden, the grapevines, the cherry tree. The imagination needs spaces; I can't think of my characters separately from the space that surrounds them. Places are as important as characters. What shapes our identity? Family, society, politics, ideas, music, books. But also the landscape, its light, its sounds and smells. My family emigrated from

Romania in 1985, but its soundtrack still plays inside me. My ancestors lived for centuries in the fascinating region below the Carpathian Mountains that we now know as Transylvania, which was given to Romania after the First World War. Emigration during the communist period and after the fall of the Iron Curtain brought an 800-year history to an end.

But has it really ended? Writing is a rebellion against time and its greatest impertinence, transience. Writers are, in part, chroniclers of their time, devoting themselves to places and objects that, as W.G. Sebald says in *Austerlitz*, cannot remember or tell of themselves. My novels are also an inventory against forgetting. I see time not as a directional force, but as juxtaposition, concurrence, as an organic web. This is how the idea arose of telling Samuel's life story through the ways in which it touched others. This open form of composition shows that everything, no matter how complex, is just an excerpt. And this in turn gives the reader a more active role. If I had one wish, it would be for you, the reader, to inhabit these places with all your senses, and to feel something of the characters' attachment to them.

What a great joy for me that my novel is now being published in the UK, by Moth Books!

Best wishes,
**Iris Wolff**

# Zăpadă

· · · · ·

Let me keep the child.

Florentine did not think these words, she did not speak them. She surrendered herself to them. They had inscribed themselves into her, become her companions. First on the cart, and then on the train to Arad, where she took a taxi from the station to the hospital. Let me keep the child, please. The words reverberated in the snow, flew up like the flakes on the road's edge, rolled along the rails with her, monotonous, fitful. The high thin whistle blew them into a warning. In the taxi the words became a knotted lump, sitting in her gullet, sitting in her stomach, her fists, her mouth. Let me, please.

It had been snowing for a week. Small, innocent-looking flakes at first, speckling the yard like an animal's back. They covered the roofs of the houses; at first it was only the steeple they slipped off. Each flake one of a kind, as if designed in a fit of exuberance and sent out to make everything disappear: surrounding villages, fields, the hills on the horizon, and finally the horizon itself. Hannes had given up shovelling the snow in the yard and concentrated on clearing one path to the road and one to the next house. He went out three times a day, resigned to the mountains of snow rising metres high on either side.

He had walked Florentine along these holloways that morning, out of the yard, across the road, past the church. A single vehicle stood on the high street, a horse and cart with sled runners. On the carter's seat, a man in a fur coat and hat, slumped as if in sleep. Florentine and Hannes exchanged a glance. She nodded. As they approached, the man righted himself. He climbed into the back, opened several wooden barrels and began extolling their contents. In one, the bodies of the fish were all pointing the same way, silvery bellies, grey-black backs, a shoal in the sea poised to change direction at any moment. In another barrel they were laid out in a star, tails to the centre, heads pointing out, dozens of heads, gills, eyes.

Hannes said what they wanted, slipped the man some money, finally even bought fish so he would take her. The fish would be thrown away. After this trip, Florentine would never again eat salted herring.

The man whipped up his horse. Hannes walked a few paces with them, as if wanting to follow the cart. Florentine looked back until the road curved and she lost sight of him. Before long, the village too had disappeared. The runners slid over the snow, the harness creaked, a little bell rang – bright, incessant – and when she touched her belly, Florentine seemed to hear a sound like glass breaking in two. Each bend in the road was a return of the last, each clump of trees a repeat of the others. There were no colours, no firm outlines, only the gliding of the cart, the bright bell ringing and the smell of salt fish. In the open country with no trees or houses to break the wind, she saw in her mind's eye the runners sliding off the side of the road. Barrels and fish tipping over, a great hand strewing them carelessly across the snow – a grey-black pattern in the constant white.

The carter did not speak. Florentine realised he was watching her from the corner of his eye, had registered the hands crossed over her belly and the way she braced herself as they went over bumps. He steered the horse down the middle of the road and slowed going into the bends – he had understood what was happening here. Between coat and fur hat, his eyes were all she could see of him. There was no telling his age, nor whether his face was handsome or shared the coarseness of his hands. Florentine was grateful. He knew these roads, could navigate by scant markers, shrubs and trees that were meaningless to her. He knew which tree marked the turn-off and avoided obstacles she spotted much too late. He had probably been travelling these roads for years, summer and winter, with his livelihood of salt fish.

And a Romanian, of all people, her father would say. But at that moment this man was closer to her than any one.

The snow brought a brightness that had put Florentine on edge in recent days, driving her from one room of the house to another – spaces that were not yet familiar. The rooms seemed to be watching them; even whispered words and small gestures would not go unnoticed, as if the house had long since formed a picture of them: a woman with freckled skin, thin, almost gangly, in flares and an embroidered camisole. A man with a full, dark beard and chin-length hair, who played football and guitar, dispatched to the country's western border to take over his first parish. A couple in their mid-twenties, who spent their evenings playing cards. Who studied the house with its many rooms, the garden with its vines, quince, peach and pear trees, just as the villagers studied them. Florentine had grown up in the city and did not know what life in the country would bring, what it would demand of her – but she would do her utmost to make this experiment succeed.

The previous afternoon, young people from the Christkind nativity play had gone from house to house. Everything happened silently. Since the snow had started falling, no gates were opening and closing, no doors slamming, no children's cries or voices calling from yard to yard. The snow banished sounds indoors, even the barking of the dogs. This would start up several times a day and every single night, set off by one dog and continuing until the howling encompassed the whole village. The noise would cease from one moment to the next, bringing a silence deeper than before. If Florentine were to name one thing that represented her new life, it would be this silence.

Florentine had followed the young people's progress from the kitchen window. Six figures swathed in white robes, barely visible amid the mountains of snow: Joseph, Mary in her bridal jewellery, two angels with sceptre and sword, ox and ass with grotesque faces and long horns. As the second angel was calling Mary into the hallway of the pastor's house, Florentine felt something hot between her legs. In the bathroom, she pulled down her trousers, and blood dripped from her thighs onto the tiled floor. The midwife gave her something to stop the bleeding. When it started again the following morning, Florentine set off at once. She wanted to get to the hospital despite the snow having cut the village off from the trainline.

On the way to the station, she thought about what Hannes would say in today's Christmas service: he who does not want to win, who gives his will over to God – he is invincible. On this day, Florentine was not invincible. She crossed her arms over her belly, pressed her thighs together and closed her eyes. But she found no darkness, just persistent white.

The fish seller waited until the train came. Only later did it occur to her that they had not exchanged a word all the way there. As the train moved off, she cleared a peephole in the fogged window. He was standing on the platform, hands in his coat pockets, face hidden by hat and collar. She nodded to him, and thought he nodded back, or perhaps just raised a hand; she'd forgotten by the time the train had left the station.

Even someone who has been the only person in the world for you could vanish, she thought, as if he'd never existed.


Amid the pleas and weeping of the women, Florentine could barely make out what the doctor at the foot of the bed was saying.

Had he really asked what she'd taken?

The doctor had a bald head and scrawny hands, which he only removed from the pockets of his white coat to blow his nose. So far, no one had examined her.

'Nothing, I've taken *nothing*. I'm here for you to save the child.'

Florentine made to get up. A nurse standing by her bed pushed her back down. Then the doctor deigned to take a look. He laid his head on her belly. She could feel his large, cold ear. Something was said, noted down, she couldn't hear what. The doctor left without a glance at the other women. The nurse handed her a bluish pill. Florentine regarded it mistrustfully, swallowed it. Then, finally, darkness.

When she woke, it was night outside the windows. She laid her hands on her belly, as she had for the past six months, flat, the fingers spread. Strange as it seemed, she could see the child, could feel his outlines. After her inner soundings, she was reassured. She put her feet on the floor and stood, reluctantly barefoot; she couldn't find her shoes. In the next bed lay a girl scarcely older than fifteen: a Transylvanian, you could tell from her nightshirt. She was unmoving, her eyes fixed on the ceiling. Beside her, a Romanian lay murmuring something to herself that sounded like a poem or a prayer. A woman too old, really, for pregnancy, sat on the edge of her bed holding her belly and rocking back and forth. Someone was crying, others chatting. Then she felt a warm, warning tingle on the back of her neck. A woman by the window was fixing her with her gaze, as if to say: stop staring at the others. Florentine sensed something in her give way. The air was stuffy. The babble of voices grew softer, became almost inaudible, yet carried on. So they had all been placed in one room on purpose. This delivered the doctors from the responsibility of seeing them as individuals; judging and condemning was easier from the foot of the bed.

She walked along the brightly lit corridor. There was no one in sight. Finally, she found something she took to be a toilet. She went in, leaned on the door and closed her eyes. Then she smelled the stench. There were no toilet bowls, just two holes in the floor. The solid structure of the room dissolved as she saw what was lying at her feet, to be sluiced with a bucket of water and swept down the drain with a broom. She saw the little arms and tiny hands barely grown, the curled spines and reptilian heads with their delicate closed eyelids, the pink skin, the bruises, the blood. Florentine just managed to lean over a sink before vomiting.

The way to end an unwanted pregnancy was to jump off the table, carry heavy things, or ask someone to punch you in the belly. The angel-makers in the village counselled high doses of sage, arnica, rosemary, parsley, mugwort or angelica. If nothing worked, you could try a weak solution of prussic acid or a knitting needle. Women who resorted to such measures risked becoming infertile.

Or they might fare as Nika had.

They had met at the town hall, waiting in a queue to see someone. Nika's theory was that the government intended queuing to keep people fit, delivering them from further sporting activity. The time gained should, in her view, be spent drinking coffee. Or a glass of vişinată – or better still, both.

Nika was Florentine's first friend in the village. They met several times a week for coffee and sour cherry liqueur. Mostly in Nika's kitchen, where the radio blared, one of her three children would be playing and there was always a cake in the oven or a pan of soup on the hob. Hannes could tell where Florentine had been from the smell. A blend of kitchen aromas, coffee and cigarette smoke.

Nika with a cigarette between her fingers, thin threads of rising smoke whirled together by the movements of her hands as they emphasised, glossed or questioned what she had to say – this was the first image that appeared when Florentine thought of her friend. Then her light-green eyes (with a look that hovered between expectation and exuberance), the quickness of her mind, her sarcasm and ready laughter, which also revealed her melancholy. A family trait, she said. Nika had been born in Bukovina, in a village where her first love had taken his own life at eighteen. Whatever you do, don't become a poet, she told her sons. They die young, and they can't say what they think, whether on this side of the forests or the other.

Florentine and Nika both fell pregnant in summer. But Nika didn't want another child. She injected herself with something you give cows, and died in three days, convulsing. At the hospital, they refused to treat her. There were no abortions in the Socialist Republic of Romania.

The doctor with the cold ear discharged Florentine at the end of the week. The bleeding had stopped, and there was nothing more they could do for her. His attitude suggested that he still suspected her of trying to end her pregnancy, but he said nothing. She was glad to be allowed home. To get out of the overcrowded room, to sleep in her own bed, take a bath, be with Hannes – who had tried to visit her, but wasn't let in, or so Mariana had heard. Mariana heard everything. Florentine had often gone over to the Roma woman's bed, and they had opened the window a crack and watched the snow drifting on the street.

Mariana wore a loose, floor-length housecoat and dangled her legs like someone sitting on a wall. She was expecting her fourth child and had been in hospital for weeks. The window bed wasn't allocated to newcomers. She knew how to get a larger portion of food, how to stop slippers from disappearing when the cleaner came round, and she showed her the lavatories that the nurses used, one floor down.

'How do you know all these things?' Florentine had inquired.

'By not asking.'

'When your son comes, walk the stairs,' Mariana advised her in parting. 'Don't let these devils tie you to the bed.'

Florentine was not surprised to hear her speak of a son. Her inner soundings had led her to the same conclusion. On the train, she laid her hands on her belly, flat, fingers spread, and focused on the boy's outlines. After a while, she realised she was going the wrong way. She got off at the next station and found herself on a deserted platform. There was no telling when the next train would come. Stations in the Banat were designed for people who didn't need to go anywhere.

The snow had stopped. The sky was a watery blue; crows drew arcs above the fields. As Florentine was breaking icicles off the roof of the shelter and putting them to her mouth, everything changed.

The blue deepened, the arcs disappeared.

She sat down on a rock and waited for a train to take her back to Arad.

Florentine followed Mariana's advice. In March, she walked doggedly up and down the stairs, one hand on the banister, the other on her belly. The nurses tried to take her back to bed, but Florentine resisted, walked down one floor, then back up, down and up again. Eventually, she knew it was enough. She lay down on the delivery bed in the labour ward and said it was starting. The birth took less than two hours. The doctor only came when they could see the baby's head.

Hannes waited outside. Visitors were not allowed, not even for a birth, not even your own husband. Despite the first signs of spring, it was cold, with patches of snow still on the ground. Winter clung on there, unreasonable, unruly.

The baby was wrapped in a cloth and laid on Florentine's breast. She could feel his heartbeat. He screamed for a moment, and then grew very quiet, and with Florentine's exhaustion, all-encompassing elation and pride, came an unexpected seriousness. So this is the boy. This and no other.

The nurses gathered at the window.

'There's a man standing on a car roof.'

Florentine smiled.

'Tell him it's a boy, and he has small ears.'

The pear trees were laden with small, hard fruit. The quinces were ripe.

Not to use every last gift from the garden, to eat it, boil it up into jam or dry it in the loft, would have been ingratitude. In their early years Florentine had tried to do it all herself (until the berries turned her hands and her dreams red). Now, her neighbours helped. These women had a way of pausing in their work, wiping hands on pinafores, palms then backs, their bodies leaning in slightly as if these few extra centimetres were needed to share a message that would otherwise be lost. Taken by the wind, snagged in the treetops.

Her silence must have given the impression that she thought herself above them. Words gave Florentine a sense of unease that could never quite be dispelled. The things people said were blurred, and it unsettled her. However hard she tried, speaking never came close to the reality of experience. She liked to let her mind wander as she plucked currants and raspberries, harvested grapes, picked apples – to listen to what the words were debating among themselves, what memories they stirred. Words had settled in an indistinct place where thinking and feeling bled into one another.

It must have been her fault that Samuel still wasn't speaking at two and a half. Florentine had kept quiet as he was growing in her belly, quiet as she walked the pram over the fields and along the river bank. Launching boats onto puddles, spending the summer in a hammock, hiding in the leaves, making snow faces with dried corncobs – their games of silence. When Samuel liked something, he showed it; he left them in no doubt when he didn't. He spoke with his laugh, his eyes, but no word had yet passed his lips, nothing that sounded like Mama or Papa or anything else that might be a child's first word.

'You need to demonstrate,' people told her.

They bent down to the boy and formed single words, over-articulating, pointing at objects.

'Ball,' they said, tongues doming in their mouths.

'Mama,' they said, pointing at Florentine, who froze under the drawn-out double syllable. Samuel looked at mouths, balls, his mother, his father, and stayed silent.

Hannes grew anxious. Florentine could wait.

She was quiet beside the chattering neighbours, concentrating on the rustle of footsteps in the leaves, the rapping of a woodpecker. Quinces were going into wicker baskets, pears into large dishes with handles, plums into enamel bowls. The sinking sun reddened sky and roof tiles alike. The garden lay in shadow. A soft breeze cooled the nape of her neck, carrying over the odd word.

Eventually one of the women held out her hands to Florentine. She studied them, and then her own.

'You're the only one with red hands.'

In the afternoon, Hannes came into the kitchen with two other men. Florentine wasn't particularly surprised; it was normal for travellers to ask to stay overnight at the pastor's house. She looked the two of them up and down. They couldn't be older than twenty, and their threadbare trousers and shoes revealed that they were travelling on foot. One man put his rucksack down and held out his hand.

'I'm Benedikt. You can call me Bene.'

'Florentine – no abbreviation.'

'Can I help?' he asked. He washed his hands and began peeling potatoes with surprising skill.

Florentine learned that the pair were trainee teachers. They came from East Germany and were hitchhiking to the Black Sea. Bene had black hair, light skin, and dimples that Florentine found both affable and rakish. His hands were beautiful, with long, slender fingers that chopped onions and garlic, diced parsley roots and celery with practised ease, while he asked questions and told stories.

What an impressive house it was, he said, with the tall gate, the surrounding wall, the many rooms and the high ceilings. And the garden! Did Florentine manage it on her own? What was the dog's name? Schopenhauer? Florentine explained that it hadn't been her idea, they had inherited him from the previous pastor. Schopenhauer wouldn't have survived a move. He was old, very old, wouldn't bark even if the house was burning down.

Bene laughed, and Florentine found that she had unwittingly fallen into a pleasant conversation with him as they cooked. Over dinner, she finally took a closer look at the man who had introduced himself as Lothar. He had dark eyes and a prominent nose that didn't really suit his face, which was otherwise made up of soft lines. His voice was husky, with an unfathomable depth. He thought before speaking, which was probably less uncertainty than a desire to say precisely what he meant. Bene, meanwhile, talked without pausing for thought, his intellect skittish, with a streak of childish boisterousness. No wonder Samuel immediately befriended him. He wanted to sit beside him at dinner and Bene was told to help Florentine put him to bed.

He read him a story, something about a wizard and a girl. Florentine lay on the side of the bed nearest the wall, drew out the boy's curls between thumb and forefinger, and breathed in the scent of his hair. Bene neither acted out the scenes nor put on voices for the different characters. His face became a calm river; even though you'd only dipped in a timid hand, it soon carried everything away. Florentine walked into this river, which had carried Samuel halfway into sleep before she noticed that Bene had also begun to stroke the foot that stuck out from under the covers. His fingers stroked Samuel's toes, the smooth skin of the heel, the calf, which retained something of babyhood. Something was always preserved, allowing a slow farewell. The softness, the smoothness, the daintiness; Florentine could see that Bene was not seeking these sensations, just absorbing them as he read.

When he laid the book aside it was a sign, and the two of them stopped touching the child.

Every morning, while the boy was still asleep, Florentine sat on the steps that led down to the back yard and the garden. Hannes could be up until after midnight, brooding over a text or a book. She couldn't go to bed early enough. When she put out the light she felt a little thrill of anticipation, hard to explain, for the moment when she would awaken.

There had been a time when the first thing in Florentine's mind in the morning was an all-encompassing 'No'. A no to her father's knock at the door, to the slippers that had slid away under the bed, to the cold of the bathroom. A no to the crockery in the sink, the jam jar that wouldn't open, the trouser hem that had come down – the great, never-ending conspiracy of things. Here, there was no less to be done. Five rooms, plus the kitchen, loft and wine cellar. A garden, chickens, cats, a decrepit dog. And yet the no was gone. The house had more rooms than she had excuses, more windows than she could close her eyes to. She had wished to be free of responsibility. But perhaps a life without obligation was the opposite of happiness.

At the residential school no weekend passed without parties. You got through the lessons, earned a little money in the afternoons, helping out in a bakery, ironing shirts. From Friday to Sunday, nights were for living. Florentine always wanted to stay out late. That was when the wildest dancing happened, when it was clear who was going home with whom, when it didn't matter who paid. The late ones had the escapades that would be talked about long afterwards: swimming in the river, shivering with cold; stealing the caretaker's keys and shouting into the night from the roof.

Her favourite drink was a bloody Mary, tomato juice with vodka, salt and pepper. A Kent to go with it; she only smoked Nationals when her money ran low. On one visit, her father found the overflowing ashtray on the window ledge. It was the wind's job to empty it. Florentine could generally recover a clean ashtray in the morning.

Her father's slap hit her without warning.

The night must have been still.

Florentine's head remained turned away, her father's hand half outstretched, as if he didn't want to take it back. You have hit me for the last time, Florentine decided. She was tired of putting up with the moods that had taken hold of him since her mother left. He had been in Russia, first in the war, and then in captivity. For a long time, her mother tried to pick up the life they'd had before, and then she left, like someone going shopping, or visiting a friend – without much luggage, without many words. Florentine knew she had tried. But perhaps she should have tried for longer, shown less forbearance, set boundaries for the small insults and for the large, unforgivable ones.

After six months Hannes asked her to marry him and move with him to the Banat. He invited her out to the coffeehouse. When she saw the flowers under the table, she knew.

Florentine sat on the back steps, as discreet as a silent guest. That youthful resistance had denied her something that was now given to her, morning after morning, something she would not have missed for the world. The trick was to appear in the garden at the same hour every day, until you were part of it and the secret no longer hid itself. Today, for the first time, there was a touch of moisture on the steps, a smattering of dark purple among the bushes. The autumn put a distance between the houses, moved them further apart. Something was taking up the space between, and Florentine was fully occupied in discovering what it was.

Bene and Lothar were sleeping. Florentine made breakfast. The last tomatoes from the garden, telemea, bread, plum jam and acacia honey, with coffee made in a pan. She ironed the Geneva bands, brushed the cassock, got herself and Samuel dressed.

The verger greeted her at the side door. The church was cool and dusky, although candles were lit. Leaning back, Florentine looked up at the stars painted on the church ceiling. Simple, black stars regularly dispersed over the white. The bells rang, the church filled up, women on one side, men on the other. Samuel was with the organist in her gallery, and it was hard to persuade him to go with Florentine as the first organ notes rang out.

The man who ascended the steps of the pulpit was not the same man with whom she shared a bed, took her meals, argued, laughed and debated. He had the power to dispense God's blessing, and Florentine rarely went to church without contemplating this difference. His voice was altered, as was his bearing. His words were emphatic, his gestures calm, and she admired how naturally he assumed this role. During the sermon her eyes travelled back to the starry sky. It had taken her some time to understand its secret. The pattern was made up of three shapes: four-pointed, six-pointed, and round, like little suns. They were spaced with a regularity that she felt was unparalleled. Every star had its place, kept its distance, and yet seemed to need the others close by. Samuel looked up, too. Their hands lay close together.

When the service was over, she and Hannes said goodbye to the parishioners. Groups lingered in conversation beneath the chestnut trees; at church you could find out everything about other people, as if by chance. It was general knowledge that Samuel couldn't speak, that Hannes liked to play football (many suspected he had only become a pastor when his dream of playing professional football failed). People knew which cow had calved and when, who was courting whom, who had a wandering eye, perhaps even when and how often the villagers made love.

By the time they were back home, it was almost midday. Schopenhauer was asleep between the gate and the front door. Stretched out as though a great weariness had overtaken him on his way from one to the other. The kitchen table was cleared, the dishes washed. Florentine knocked on the door beside Hannes' study. Without thinking, she went in. She picked up a guidebook for Rome, flicked absently through it, looked around the room – half-full water glasses, towels and a sun hat on the bed – and felt she had to commit it all to memory, as if she risked overlooking something, as if what she was searching for (was she searching for anything?) were obscure, hidden. The guest room looked as it always did: double bed, table, chairs, a stool that served as a bedside table, a spherical ceiling light, a cupboard with green shimmering glass inserts, reflecting her face. She put the book back and only then noticed something placed inside. Between the Trevi Fountain and the Piazza Navona was a vine leaf. Samuel had handed Bene something from every corner of the garden, twigs, flowers, nuts, a vine leaf, and Florentine had let Bene know that he could discreetly make the gifts disappear.

She found the two men on a blanket by the well.

Bene's head rested on Lothar's thighs.

Feeling like an intruder, Florentine called them in for lunch a little awkwardly, from a distance.

After the meal, Hannes fell asleep with Samuel on the sofa. Bene and Lothar were in the garden, having promised to gather plums. Florentine began to tidy the room, then changed her mind. She packed up a cake and a dozen pears, took her blue coat from the peg.

The house was on the road out of the village.

Always when she walked this way, the bright sound of a bell seemed to accompany her. Colours faded, the fields gave off a salty scent and with eyes closed, she saw silver-black fish in the snow.

Paul opened the door. Since Nika's death his face was this: solemn eyes with shadows no sleep, sun or fresh air could banish. As she passed him, he briefly touched her arm – his way of greeting her.

Mirko was playing in the living room. Thea was asleep and Oswald, the youngest, was in the garden. Florentine watched him from the window. He was turning apples laboriously in his hand, checking for worms.

'How are you?'

The mind took time; the heart was quick.

She could see how he was.

Paul was dealing with his own grief. Mirko had already started school, Thea was independent, but Oswald (the same green eyes as his mother, the same expression of sadness and warmth) was a worry. None of the children had been allowed to go to Nika as she lay dying. But Oswald had hidden under the table in her room. He had wanted to put his hands on his mother's belly, as she had always done for him when his tummy hurt.

The kitchen table held a jigsaw puzzle, newspapers, plates of half-eaten soup. Clothes were draped on the backs of chairs, and the range had a greasy sheen. Otherwise, little had changed since the days when Florentine used to sit here with Nika and their coffee, liqueur and cigarettes. The radio wasn't playing. It wasn't on the windowsill. Some things Paul had left as they were, and others had disappeared very quickly: the radio, the plants. A year after her death, Nika's light pink dressing gown still hung on the bathroom door. Eventually, Florentine took it away, without asking.

Oswald came in and showed his father the basket of apples. Paul reminded him to greet Florentine. The boy said hello without looking at her. Only one woman had had a right to this room, a woman with green eyes and boundless laughter, and perhaps that was the reason why Paul wanted to remain alone.

She began to tidy up.

'You don't need to…,' said Paul.

'I know.'

He came over as if to stop her, but there was no conviction in it, more a desire for closeness.

In the morning, Florentine sat on the steps at the usual hour, though the night had been a short one.

It turned out that Bene and Lothar also liked playing cards. Lothar's style was strategic and humourless. But Bene did his utmost to glimpse the others' hands (an unobtrusive trip to the sink, a feigned coughing fit), to get himself and Florentine the highest score. Hannes was riled by the dishonesty, though it amused Florentine, who didn't really care about winning.

Bene restored peace by giving Hannes a cassette of the last Beatles album. It was the last in both senses; the band had since split up. Hannes took the cassette case, speechless, incredulous; the band's name was handwritten with a tall B and low-hanging T. The only problem was: he didn't have a cassette player.

Florentine fetched cooked tomato juice from the larder and mixed it with vodka.

'To old times,' she said.

'To love,' said Bene.

Love was better than old times, she thought, waking the next morning with a heavy head and a dry mouth.

The village would gossip about the light in the pastor's house staying on so late again. People always found something to talk about. There had been much ado about Hannes' beard. Then when he shaved it off, they had suddenly 'got used to it'. Everywhere his naked face was criticised; he was advised to eat fish and eggs, which were healthy and promoted hair growth. The regrowth of the beard was a public matter, and soon settled. Jesus's beardless appearance in Michelangelo's Last Judgement could not have caused more of a stir or garnered more criticism. Hannes complied. Florentine was less compliant. She clung to her independence. Thankfully, the days were over when she could plot the graph of her popularity by the state of the chickens each household had to offer up to the pastor.

For a long time, she had yearned to be part of this place. Eventually, she thought, she would have moved unnoticed from the edge to the centre. She would go to church on Sundays and all the other holidays. Bake cakes and slaughter the chickens whose necks the bell-ringer still wrung, because she couldn't bring herself to do it. She would go visiting with Samuel, instead of lying with him under the peach tree or walking in the fields. But how easy it was to deceive yourself. Time had passed and the things you believed in and wished for had long since become something else.

There was no centre for her and no belonging. She feared she had made her child her ally. Something would come back to this place for all time or would depart – the direction of travel couldn't be determined. The standard of happiness was set here, the standard of freedom that was necessary. That standard would inevitably slip, something that Samuel would have to discover for himself.

What would he remember? The cool metal of the wheelbarrow, where she sat him when she was busy in the garden. The taste of Nova grapes, the hard skins he spat into her hand. The scent of the honeysuckle growing up the back wall of the house. The corridor with the draughty windows, the kitchen larder from which they regularly shooed mice. The afternoons with neighbours, when everyone spoiled him, and the discipline imposed on him in church. The guests who stayed in the house from June to September, the way the Romanians and Slovakians spoke, their standard German or Banat dialect – or perhaps other things entirely, things she didn't notice and couldn't see.

Florentine sat on the steps, cooled her forehead with a glass of water, and felt a presentiment of parting. Or perhaps it was just tiredness. She looked at the vines, the whitewashed leaves, the peach and quince trees, and realised once more that something was taking refuge between them. It came to her that autumn was bringing this something, was hiding it so that it could be found again in spring. Colours that would soon vanish, or the light, and the warmth that had enveloped her in the summer months like an embrace.

She saw at this moment that Bene was standing by the well. He thought himself unobserved as he slipped out of his shirt and underpants. Florentine could not decide whether she felt ashamed or thrilled at the sight. He had a small behind, white and firm, with a darker skin tone above. Lothar caressed

Bene, scarcely more than an accidental touch that became a greater tenderness, encompassing shoulders, back and arms – and only then did Bene turn, slowly, to kiss him.

Lothar pulled up the bucket of water. They splashed each other, ducked, wrestled with restrained strength. Bene was laughing. His face wore an expression of raw defencelessness that was hardly distinguishable from pain.

Florentine wanted to stand up and did not. She stayed on the steps and watched the two men washing in the morning light.

At the start of November, a flock of sheep came to graze outside the village. At first, Samuel watched the flock from a safe distance. Then he approached a few sheep on its margins. They let him stroke them as if they hadn't noticed he was there. The dog snuffled Samuel's outstretched hand, then left him alone. Soon Florentine had to be careful she didn't lose sight of Samuel among the sheep. By the end of the week she was sitting down with the shepherd, sharing bread and cheese as if that were only natural. She was pleased to find he was not overly fond of conversation.

One afternoon, Paul joined them with Oswald and Thea.

The children ran among the flock.

Florentine and Paul leaned on a fence, watching the sheep drift in their oblivious grazing.

From time to time, someone would say something.

Getting dark early now.

Or: It's cold today.

Florentine liked these observations. Small reassurances that justified and preserved the silence.

Whenever she looked up, the sheep were distributed differently across the meadow. But if you kept your eyes on them, they didn't seem to move at all. A tractor drove over the fields, mist muffling the engine noise. From somewhere, the bright sound of a bell reached them. Florentine was gripped by unease, a sudden anxiety. The moment the dog barked, she started running. Samuel, Oswald and Thea were standing close together, staring at the ground. Oswald picked something up. The children retreated as if some creature had stepped into their midst. 'Bang!' Oswald shouted, pointing the muzzle of a pistol at Thea.

'No,' cried Paul. 'Don't!'

The sheep scattered.

Samuel glanced up, then threw his whole weight against his friend.

Oswald staggered and fell.

Florentine knelt down beside him.

The boy was lying on the ground, stiff and unmoving, one hand on his stomach, the other arm still extended as if aiming. Florentine loosened his grip and lifted him up; in her arms he grew very light.

Paul tried to say something, but she shook her head.

And while Thea began to cry, as if only the adults' reaction had shown her something had happened, Samuel stroked a sheep's woolly coat without moving his eyes from Oswald and his mother.

Paul picked up the pistol. It was loaded.

'Do you think this is a good idea?' asked Hannes, as she washed the grass stains out of Samuel's clothes that evening.

'The sheep will be gone soon,' said Florentine, 'and then we'll find something else.'

'Some occupation where the boy will learn to talk, perhaps.'

Florentine scrubbed the trousers a little harder.

She did not mention the pistol.

She stayed at home for a few days, scattered leaves and compost on the soil, horse and cow dung around the pruned roses. She and Samuel built a winter shelter for hedgehogs out of wood, brushwood and leaves, protected the pot plants from the coming frost.

A letter arrived from Bene.

In his clear, slightly rounded handwriting, he told them of his first teaching placement and invoked memories of late summer. He mentioned Lothar only once, using words so filled with love that it was clear: he knew that they knew. The planned stopover had turned into three weeks. They had bathed in the Marosch, split firewood, helped with the harvest and preparing meals. They had lain by the well and set off back to Berlin for the start of term.

It felt, said Hannes, as if the two of them were still here on a blanket in the garden, all wishes concentrated in this narrow rectangle.

When Florentine went back into the fields with Samuel, a boy was waiting for her in place of the shepherd. He sat reading on a rock. Florentine supposed that it was the shepherds first and foremost who spread Romanian literature through the country. Sheep were sacred in Romania. There were plenty of horses here, buffalo and cows, too, but only sheep had songs and poems written about them.

The boy raised a hand to his cap in greeting.

There is someone who is dreaming of something else, she thought.

Florentine seldom ventured to draw conclusions about anything beyond herself. Others had opinions; she had only the sum of many, often contradictory experiences. She doubted whether a person became wiser, despite all their insights, wise enough to judge others. Something did not change, seemed to be present from the beginning, and Samuel, who had lost himself among the sheep, daily reminded her of this.

Florentine inspected the grey of the horizon. The village looked remote. The willows dark, the fields faded. She hoped it would be a while before winter banished life back indoors and the snow came, and the storms, and she would have to plug the gaps around doors and windows with rags and newspaper.

When she asked the boy if he would be here again next year, he shrugged, vague, amicable.

Samuel was stretched out on the ground beside a yearling.

'We have to go.'

He didn't move, so she picked him up. A movement ran through the flock. Samuel and Florentine raised their eyes.

There was the grey of the sky.

The river and the willows.

The vast plain and the solitude.

There was the edge and the centre.

The yes and the no.

The uncertainty.

And yet, thought Florentine, this landscape lets you be who you are.

Snowflakes detached themselves from the grey. They fell silently on Florentine's coat, pearled into droplets on Samuel's face, and he said a word with three 'a's, two dull and one ringing, so loud and clear that the wind could not carry it away.

'Zăpadă.'

# Echo

. . . . .

There was a time that hurried forwards, and a time that ran backwards. A time that went in circles, and one that did not move, that was never more than a single moment.

Finding yourself at home in a book, scoring a decisive goal in a football game, the sun allotting you a place in the garden – that was momentary time, the time Hannes sought, preferring it to the kind that lined up the hours, days and weeks one after another, as if the point was to get somewhere.

For Ruth and Severin, time was running backwards. It stretched out into the past, so far that it threatened to snap. Their son had drowned in the Marosch. A tree trunk floating downstream had struck him on the head. Arms spread, back arched, eyes open. From the middle of the river, everything looked different: the willows, the sky, the clouds. With the view came the underwater noise: a laughter that blocked everything out, the dog barking, the friends calling out from the bank. Where he had sat with them, a semicircle of bare-chested boys, talking about school, girls, their work in the wheat and maize fields. Through which they had chased one another, parting the cucuruz stems, the leaves, the cobs. Which had been their lunch, too, polenta with milk, all at one table: Echo, his sister, their mother, their father. Who had called him a good-for-nothing that morning for the listless way he was strewing straw, wood shavings and sawdust on the floor of the byre, pausing again and again, one hand on the rake, one in his trouser pocket. Where his mother had earlier tucked a handkerchief embroidered with his monogram, a full-bellied 'B' for the family name and a curled 'G'. Gregor, his Christian name, after his grandfather, who had taught him to lie on the water like a leaf, like a stick of wood, because it had saved the old man in the war, when he floated in the open sea for two days. And Gregor had liked this floating, when his grandfather taught him to swim. When he was a little boy. When he still was.

Many others had drowned in the Marosch. Where many drowned, the likelihood of your own death seemed diminished. No one would walk away, even for a minute, from a young child playing on the bank; they would not go in the river after it had rained; and now, for some time to come, they would not float in the water, arms spread, back arched.

Hannes hesitated to enter Ruth and Severin's house. He knew that no prepared words would help, only what emerged in the moment. In seven years, he had buried three people who had drowned; Echo was the fourth. He didn't know what was worse, the drowned or those who took their own lives. In the countryside, there were many. They jumped from the roof or into the well, took a rope or the road to the trainline. Relatives tried to make it seem like an accident, and even when the facts were clear, everyone played along, even Hannes.

The gate was ajar, and chickens were running around the yard. Someone must have left the pen open. Behind the henhouse and several almond trees lay the byre; Hannes remembered Severin claiming that his cows dreamed. One heifer in particular had to be fetched in from the fields every day. While all the other animals found their own way into the village and turned off at the right yard, she stayed behind, and Severin was mocked for making such a fuss of this young cow, who clearly wasn't right in the head.

Severin had not taken off his work boots. Ruth was wearing a long, black dress. She moved so carefully she seemed to be hovering above the floor.

'He's in the next room.'

In the front parlour one cupboard remained; the other furniture had been moved out, the mirror draped with a dark cloth. Death must not find itself there, must not double itself, and the same went for the grief on your own face.

Hannes was used to how dead people looked, but when he saw the boy – the shallow chest, the dent in his skull where the tree trunk had struck him, the blank face from which something had so clearly withdrawn – he knew that everything he did was not for this body; it was for the living. Echo had always been pale, a sallowness that pooled around the eyes. Their lids were unnaturally waxy, the skin thin as paper. Tiredness was always the first thing Hannes thought of when he encountered Echo; a terrible incurable tiredness. This wan, unmoving face could display boundless joy or deep sadness, and yet reverted always to an expression of boredom. Echo's smile was stand-offish, sometimes bashful, and despite his sixteen years had still been the smile of a little boy. His gestures seemed reticent, controlled. Sometimes a crack opened up in that reserve, and then it was clear why he imposed it on himself: not because he was incapable of sympathy, far from it. His face betrayed everything. Anyone could read his thoughts there, and so it had taken something beyond self-control to hide them.

Hannes said a prayer. Then he blessed Echo.

The dispassion with which Ruth straightened the shirt that was already straight, arranged the trouser hem that was already arranged, was painful. She moved slowly, as if there were a great distance between the decision to raise her arm and the actual movement of her fingers. Echo's sister was sitting on a chair by the window, though Hannes only saw her when he turned to leave the room. He nodded but couldn't tell if she noticed.

In the hall, Ruth stopped.

'He keeps on drinking and working as if nothing's happened.'

It took Hannes a moment to realise she was talking about her husband.

'He hasn't even been to see the boy.'

She was angry, but her gestures were muted, and Hannes couldn't help but notice the beauty of this self-imposed restraint, the same as Echo's.

'Give him time. He's doing what's right for him. That doesn't mean he isn't grieving just as you are.'

He couldn't understand her failure to see Severin's suffering. The thing that helped you wasn't necessarily right for someone else.

Once they had discussed the funeral, he went with Severin to the byre. Not because he'd planned to, just because he had followed him out and Hannes couldn't bear to leave him alone.

The stalls smelled of straw, butyric acid, a hint of vanilla. Thirteen cows, six on one side and seven on the other, all bending over the feed trough. Only one heifer, scarcely more than twelve months old, with a strangely colourless hide, stood with her head raised, not moving as they stopped in front of her, not even flicking her ears to shoo away the flies. Her eyes shone. Losing himself in that bottomless black, Hannes knew, without a doubt, that this animal dreamed.

He cycled home. It wasn't far, but on foot he would have had to greet people, exchange a few words and – even if he turned the invitation down – he'd find himself in someone's yard. There was always something to discuss, always a need for consolation or advice, and an especially good wine they were obliged to offer to the pastor.

He heard the wind before he felt it. Like footsteps taking a run-up – but it was only the wind corralling the early fallen leaves. Head down, weight on the pedals. In summer there was no coat collar to turn up, no hat to pull over your forehead; you were at the wind's mercy. Wind that scattered dust into your eyes, hurt your ears, tousled your hair. Wind that swept roof tiles off the houses, rattled shutters, slammed doors. That blew out candles without warning, turned the pages of books, snatched up newspapers.

A great, capricious breath.

Storks taking flight from an electricity pylon, as if the wind was lifting them out of their nest, awoke the memory of the parish where Hannes had finished his training. A village with more storks than human inhabitants. He missed the church fortress on the Zibin River, the lanes with their Roman numerals, which had names only in the vernacular – above all he missed the Carpathian Mountains. Their presence altered the light. At midday it was a greenish violet (in winter, silvery blue), and in the afternoon a golden yellow that spilled over into copper as evening fell. Every morning, the mountains washed out the colours anew.

The Banat had felt like a punishment to him. But you don't resist a call. Here, summers were dry and dusty, winters lost in the endless white of the plain. There were no mountains to wash the light, to break the wind.

His wife lived here with an ease he had not been granted in all these years. Perhaps because she had her routine and was self-sufficient, imperturbable, barely needing reassurance from people or places. Florentine was always occupied, even if her occupation wasn't obvious. She disappeared with Samuel into the garden or the fields, left the house after lunch and didn't return until evening. Without exception she woke early, sat on the back steps, and convinced the morning of its presence.

He had always liked this vague, intangible quality and still did. And yet he had to take care not to begrudge Florentine her independence, not to blame her for the boy being as quiet as she was.

Samuel had learned to speak late, a mix of dialect-inflected German, Romanian and Slovakian. He was shaped by his parents, the bell-ringer Rositante, who slaughtered chickens, helped with the cleaning and made an effort to speak standard German, the gardener Ovidiu, who mowed the grass, split wood, repaired wine barrels and yet always looked idle; by whist partners Konstanty and Malva and their daughter Stana. A serious girl with watchful eyes and pupils scarcely bigger than pinpricks. Because of this friendship, Samuel counted in Slovakian: jeden, dva, tri, štyri, päť, šesť, sedem, osem, deväť, desať. Hannes recited German numbers time and again, but he had to admit there was a musicality to the Slovakian ones that made them easier to learn.

School would begin in a few weeks but, unlike other children, Samuel was not looking forward to it. The entire congregation knew to avoid the subject, and hardly anyone let slip the word 'school'. Samuel could not be forced to do something against his will. He was a fussy eater; there were days when he asked for precisely ten (desať!) peas, no more, no less, only ate unblemished apples or plums he had picked himself.

Florentine was the only person Samuel permitted to dress and bathe him and put him to bed. Hannes might sometimes be tolerated as a reader but never became part of the elaborate ceremony that began with tooth-brushing and ended with a goodnight kiss. His greatest disappointment, however, was that he could not spark a love of football in his son. He had made a goal out of planks and an old fishing net, practised passing and combination play with the boy, tackles, shooting, trained him as a goalkeeper; nothing ignited even a fraction of his own passion. Samuel obliged him, standing in goal and saving balls competently, but listlessly. After the game he sought refuge in one of the neighbours' yards. Samuel was allowed to go wherever he liked, and Hannes feared he was being spoiled, which Florentine firmly denied.

'Life will be hard enough when he's older,' she said. 'Let him have this time.' And she looked at him as if thinking, why do I have to explain this to you?

Hannes had wanted a lot of children. But life didn't owe you anything, least of all the fulfilment of your desires. After two miscarriages, Florentine had reached an acceptance that for him remained distant. They hardly spoke about it. Perhaps one of the secrets of their marriage was that neither insisted on things. He didn't ask where she went, Florentine never pinned him down – and so gave him the sense that he could be anything.

He was the eldest of three brothers and had felt even as a boy that he had to make something of himself. But what? Every person should be born with a user manual, a laundry label, setting out a rough, a very general direction to follow and other care instructions. For a long time he had failed to wrest any direction from life – had tried football and music before studying theology – always aware of his duty to succeed. If only for the sake of his mother Karlina, whose life, begun in a grand villa, had dwindled to a button-factory conveyor belt.

When Hannes arrived home, the house and garden were deserted. Even Ovidiu, who had begun to trim the hedges, was not there. Already the hedges were angular instead of round. If he sent Ovidiu out for grape juice, he would take so long it was wine by the time he returned. If he asked him to beat nuts out of the tree, he would start with the plums. Ovidiu did as he pleased, as Hannes had learned when he gave him his first task. Hannes wanted a garden shed, described how it should look, even made a drawing. When the shed was finished, its sole window was on the opposite side to the one Hannes had stipulated.

It was wiser for the window to face the yard gate, Ovidiu said. After all, you needed to see who was coming to visit.

Hannes took his guitar to the bench by the shed. The door was ajar; through the crack came the smell of discarded wine barrels and engine oil. His fingers stiffened up when he hadn't played for a while, and it took some time to dispel the voice that said there was no point when you had so little talent.

It will do for your confirmands, he argued back.

Patches of lawn had been trodden away; no grass grew around the dog kennel, either. Why he hadn't dismantled it after all these years, he couldn't say. The vines looked like they'd been dusted with flour. A sallow white like the boy's paper skin. Rust patiently continued devouring the iron gate. The chestnut trees were as tall as the church roof. A cloud had snagged on the steeple.

His gaze slipped down it.

He stopped playing only when the wind started up again. There is a devil in every wind, as Romanians say.

Today, it was doubt.

In the evening, while Florentine was putting Samuel to bed, Hannes sat on the back steps with his notes and a glass of wine. The sun had set. Dusk had settled over the garden. But above the roofs the light held on, granting a respite, a delay, a sojourn.

A few workable thoughts for his sermon, and then he faltered: too much 'one should' and 'we must'. Anyone who speaks in the name of others is an imposter, he had read in Cioran. A writer has responsibility only for himself.

Hannes had a recurring dream.

He woke up in bed, but despite all efforts of will and strength, could not move or speak. He was trapped in his body, which lay still and passive. The body did not obey him or belong to him as it usually did. When he was typing, there was no saying how the order for a small 'e' or a capital 'L' arrived, what conveyed the letters so quickly that the clacking keys could keep pace with the speed of his thoughts. You could hold a cup and forget it at the same time, ride a bicycle while your mind was elsewhere. The senses that apprehended everything, that helped him find his bearings in a strange place or another face – they were gone. It was frightening.

He recalled dreams in which he was standing on ice, the depths of a frozen lake beneath him, dreams in which he had to swim through milky, cloudy pools that stretched endlessly ahead. But this paralysis was new. He could see through his closed eyelids, could feel Florentine beside him, oblivious, and the abandonment, the loneliness of that was worse than anything he had ever known.

Thinking of Echo was like a foretaste of this paralysis.

'How are Ruth and Severin doing?'

Florentine sat down beside him on the steps and lit a cigarette.

'They're not talking to each other.'

Hannes filled the glass she held out.

'And it's hard for me to find the right words, too. Do I tell them that dying so young has meaning, that they'll see Echo again one day?'

'Isn't that what you believe?'

Hannes fixed his eyes on a point in the twilight. The moment of deferral was over; now everything was vanishing quickly, the light, the warmth.

'Belief is grace. You can't just want to believe, that would be ridiculous. I can't imagine that the other side is a place where we simply reappear, that we'll recognise each other like we do in the street.'

'How do you know they want to hear that?' Florentine asked. 'I don't envy you. But you must find something to comfort them. And it won't be your self-pity.'

'One point to you.'

'It's not about winning.'

Though Florentine didn't say things out of a desire to reproach him or justify herself, her words could still sting. They came out haphazardly, at random, as if they had a life of their own – she seldom managed to align what she thought and what she said, a thing that came naturally to others. Hannes tried not to hold it against her. He had learned to cope with this, to provide context for himself or for others, to take away or add something, as seemed necessary.

Sometimes it worked. Sometimes it went awry.

Like the business with Konstanty Novac.

The village was home to a few Protestant Slovakians. The Novacs had come to see Hannes five years earlier, to have their daughter Stana baptised. Since then, whist evenings with them had become a regular fixture. Florentine had made friends with Malva and Samuel with Stana. No one had made friends with Konstanty, an impulsive, uncomfortably inquisitive character.

Certain topics were skirted in his presence. Certain conversations were only to be had in the open air; your own house might have ears. Over time, the list of topics to be skirted grew and grew, which didn't make things easier – but after five years of whist evenings, they couldn't put a stop to them without some kind of explanation.

One evening in early July, Konstanty had dropped by alone, just when some East German visitors happened to be there. Because centuries back after the dissolution of the monasteries Luther had instructed all pastors to continue the tradition of hospitality, not a week went by without visitors. Most were passing through Arad and Deva on their way to Hermannstadt, and would stop off for a few days. Since Bene and Lothar, no one had stayed for weeks; all the same, Hannes and Florentine suspected the pair of having advertised their services. An unusual number of trainee teachers from Berlin had come to visit. To begin with guests stayed in the house, then when it became too much for Florentine they camped in the garden, until someone gave Hannes to understand that 'certain people' frowned upon it. From that time on, visitors set up camp by the Marosch, and only came to the pastor's house to eat or bathe.

They had not heard the footsteps in the corridor, or the door opening (perhaps he had not even knocked) when Konstanty was suddenly standing in the kitchen. He was obviously drunk.

Florentine was the first to react.

'Dobrý večer, Konstanty.'

Konstanty came to the table and eyed the things on it: cigarettes, matches, newspapers. Then he eyed the students. Hannes lit a cigarette and took another from the pack. Konstanty accepted the offered light and went to the window, where he took off his hat and smoked in silence. Hannes watched his face reflected in the windowpane.

'Won't you sit down?'

Konstanty turned.

'I'd much rather know who your visitors are.'

Hannes gave the students a look.

The three said their names.

'Hans, Klaus or Helmut, it's all the same to me,' said Konstanty from the window seat. 'What brings hordes of you out here, and what do you have to talk about, that's what I'd like to hear.'

Hannes got up to fetch another glass from the sideboard. Midway, he paused. He heard Florentine's voice.

'Don't. Konstanty has had enough to drink. He's going to go home now, he'll accept our hospitality another time.'

Konstanty's eyes narrowed. The student sitting between Florentine and the window ducked, as if to dodge a blow. Konstanty teetered, caught himself, went to the table. He stubbed out the cigarette, slowly, his gaze travelling from one to another before settling on Florentine. Then he walked out. His hat still lay on the window seat.

The following afternoon, Hannes received an invitation to the police station. He was led down to the cellar.

It was more comfortable downstairs, a policeman said.

Hannes took a seat in a windowless room. A circle of light fell on the tabletop. Following instructions, he placed his hands in the circle, palms down. Three other people were present, one asking questions, one writing, the third silent behind him.

Hannes answered the questions which, when they were finished, started again from the beginning.

Why the visits, and what did they talk about.

Hannes resolved to stay calm, choosing to say too little rather than too much. When asked if they spoke about politics, he could honestly say no. Why did so many guests come? He didn't know. No, he didn't intend to stop them coming. Eventually, he lost all sense of time. He felt he had been sitting in this room for days, back straight, hands in the circle of light, until his beard grew down through the tabletop.

The man who had been sitting behind him – a man with a plump face and an incongruously cosy cardigan – rounded the table, tapped the lamp, seemed bored. The light swung above the tabletop. This room was in the belly of a ship. The ship was on the high seas. The sea was in a water glass. The water glass was in this room.

Hannes asked for something to drink, which aroused general mirth. He thought how easy it was to define empathy: if someone is suffering, he feels what I do when I am suffering.

When had these people mislaid their empathy?

Another man joined them. He had sleek blond hair; his summer trousers, shirt and waistcoat matched and gave him the appearance of being on a holiday – no, a grand tour.

Well, you seem to be worth the manhours, thought Hannes. Or else they aren't busy and are hoping to be entertained.

The blond man sat down beside him and told a colleague to get him a glass of water.

'You can get everything off your chest here,' he said. 'We know all about it anyway.'

'All about what?'

The man smiled.

'Drink,' he said.

Hannes drank.

'Make yourself comfortable,' said the man.

And Hannes took his hands off the table.

He could understand it, said the blond man, the rebellion, the reluctance; the Germans had suffered a certain amount of injustice. But they could still work together, for the country's future. Țară fericită, he said. Among other things.

Hannes had the distinct impression that he knew the man. His soigné appearance, the watery-pale eyes, the measured movements awakened a memory. In winter, someone he hadn't seen since his theology degree had asked to meet him. They had gone to a pub in Arad. Late in the evening, the door opened and a blond man in civilian clothes came in, accompanied by an armed soldier. Three or four other tables were occupied, all couples. Later Hannes realised that they'd all had to show their papers, everyone but him and his friend.

That was him, thought Hannes. He knew who you were, even then.

He was working towards a happy future for the country, said Hannes, in his own way.

And what way was that?

By being there for people, with their worries and hardships.

What worries and hardships specifically?

You're talking too much, thought Hannes, better to hold your tongue.

After a long silence, in which the only sounds were their breathing and a ticking of unknown origin, the man said: 'I will prepare a declaration for you to sign.'

'What kind of declaration?'

'That in your conversations with foreigners, you do not compromise respect for the Romanian state.'

The blond man squeezed his forearm, a comradely gesture, hard enough to leave no doubt about who was in charge. Then he left the room.

Hannes couldn't place him. His familiar manner, the genteel figure he cut did not fit here. Yet Hannes had the impression that of them all, he was the most well-disposed towards him.

Only one other man remained. He sat behind Hannes, the wood of his chair creaking as if in constant motion, but Hannes did not turn round. From behind a wall the ticking grew louder. Time was passing – though in this room it was most firmly suspended. Time was upstairs. Time was for other people. Now his wife and son were sitting at the kitchen table. Now they were looking at the empty chair where he usually sat. Now Samuel was undressing, leaping onto the bed, Florentine was shaking out the covers, the boy was closing his eyes, laughing. Now she lay beside him, looking for the place where she had left off and reading, one hand holding the book, the other stroking his hair. Now he was asleep, but for a long time she would stay there, half under the covers, motionless, devoted, watching his silent face.

All this went on while he was here, further away than he had ever been, so far that a seamless return to life outside this cellar became impossible. Settle in, said an inner voice, things will carry on without you, your absence carries no weight.

The door opened.

'Hands on the table,' a voice ordered.

Hannes knew this was an act, a rehearsed sequence of friendliness, threat, fear. When once more they asked what he discussed with visitors, he lost his patience.

He took his hands from the table and said: 'What do *you* speak to your visitors about, comrade? Who do you let into *your* house? Let's get the three of them down here. Or are you afraid that spying on travellers might not go down well in East Germany?'

'Save the sermon for your church, preacher. We ask the questions here.'

It ended with him having to sign the transcript of the interrogation without reading it first, and with the instruction to report on all future visits using his registered typewriter. Hannes waited for another invitation to the police station, for compliance visits, for harassment, but he was spared anything more. It might have been the mayor protecting him. It might have been Malva reminding her husband Konstanty about the matter of their friendship.

The hatred he had encountered in that windowless room stayed with Hannes. They detected and punished supposed misdemeanours with such dedication, their direction only one way, as if to distract from their own misery and shortcomings. This, then, was what it supposedly meant to work for a secure future. Justice. A system that depended on everyone being guilty.

There was only For or Against.

Bell ringing was an art.

The bells revealed the denomination of the deceased, whether a woman, a man or a young person was being buried. They set the length of the vigil, reminded people to dress for the funeral, gave the sign for the cortège to set off for the cemetery. An hour before the funeral, the small bell rang, half an hour before, the big bell, a quarter of an hour before, both at once: then it was time to leave the house.

When the funeral was that of a young person, like Echo, all the church bells rang. The tolling began at the Lutheran church, and then the other churches joined in, across all rooftops and all denominations, the reformed, the orthodox, the Greek Catholic.

The windows in Ruth and Severin's house had been opened, the chairs turned upside down. Death must not feel at home here again too soon. Samuel walked among the rearing chair legs, helped to carry wreaths and flowers into the yard; he and his friend Oswald counted the calls of a cuckoo that had strayed into the garden. The two boys remained untouched by the adults' solemn mood.

Echo was laid out in the yard, face barely discernible from pillow; only his hands stood out against the dark suit. Ruth made an effort to shoo the flies away. Someone placed a tub of iced water beneath the coffin.

Hannes consulted the head of the church council and the church warden. The latter had become reserved with him, almost unfriendly, since word got out that the young pastor had played a tape of Black Sabbath in confirmation classes to address the temptation of evil. Hannes could live with the elders criticising him, as long as he could spark enthusiasm for religion in the young.

The family gathered outside the house, Ruth and Severin, grandparents, uncles and aunts, cousins. Echo's sister wore white like all the girls. Those in mourning wear black; those celebrating life and resurrection, white. The absence of colour seemed strange against the garden's natural blue-green bunting; the black and white radiated an objectivity, a clarity, a truth usually found only in letters on paper. The outrage of death thus became an objective fact. How else could it be endured.

Florentine and Samuel went to stand with Paul and his children. An undeniable feeling of affront flashed through Hannes. They look like a family, he thought. A large family, with something to set against all the fleeting phenomena of which life is made up. Florentine pulled a thin scarf over her hair, tying it at the nape of her neck. She caught Hannes' eye and, as the bells fell silent, gave him a barely perceptible nod.

Family and friends stepped up to say farewell. At one time, everyone had been included in this leave-taking, anyone the dead person had ever said 'Good day' to in the street. Hannes was glad this had been abolished, so the time to lay a linen cloth over the dead person's head was not put off so long. Blue-tinged flies walked over Echo's face, which would never again show a rapid succession of feelings – pride, uncertainty, a little narcissism, in keeping with his age – returning at last to that look of indifference that had always distanced him slightly from the others.

Hannes could see Echo in church, his hymn book closed. He knew many hymns off by heart; he only needed to hear them once. Echo on the football field could recognise the dynamics of the game, guess what the others were planning, help his teammates think; he was in the right place at the right time, tricking his opponent, light, almost effortless. Echo on the bench in front of the house, legs outstretched, a stalk of grass between his lips. Arms spread and back arched in the river. The tree trunk came closer, and here came the feeling from Hannes' dream: he writhed and struggled, and although he wanted to warn him, no sound came from his mouth.

The coffin was nailed shut, a pitiless noise. The gravediggers asked permission to carry the dead boy out. Hannes was relieved when the bells set the funeral cortège in motion. Two of Echo's schoolfriends carried the cross, followed by Hannes, the warden and head of the church council, coffin, mourners, and finally the band.

The cemetery lay beyond the train tracks. It was a long way in the heat of the summer day. When everyone was gathered at the graveside, Severin laid the family's wreath on the coffin. The other wreaths would be placed on the grave mound later. They were made of paper. There were no flowers to be bought, and fir sprigs were rare in this part of the world. Hannes said the creed and the Lord's Prayer. The coffin was lowered in silence, then came the never-ending shovelling of earth into the grave. Finally, they sang hymn three hundred and eighty-eight which the head of the church council had announced in a fit of linguistic confusion as trei sute eighty-eight. In the hymn, the deceased comforted those who wept for him. Be not downhearted, he told them, night follows day.

On the way back, rain set in. A fine, misty drizzle; Hannes would have liked to find a name for it. For the moment, it dispelled the bleariness that had taken hold inside him. Was it the effort it had cost him to use Echo's birth name, Gregor, which felt strange on his lips? Or something else, a feeling that had not left him since the interrogation? When he heard footsteps behind him in the street, he thought: these footsteps are coming for you. When he sat at the kitchen table, it was as if his hands once more lay in the circle of light. When he had to write reports – on the visits, the conversations, all above board, all harmless, but not too trivial – he was glad not to have to use his mother tongue. One language was not plagued by prohibitions and ideological clichés; one language remained in which the words meant what they said.

'When it rains, they say the dead man is sorry for his life,' said Florentine.

She had taken off the scarf and was carrying it loosely in her hand.

Hannes thought that Echo was no longer sorry for anything.

Once those who came in for coffee had dispersed, only the closest relatives and friends remained to eat paprikash (along with the inevitable percentage who attended rituals for that reason). Florentine helped in the kitchen, washing glasses, slicing gherkins, filling plates with biscuits. Samuel acted out

*Ivanhoe*, with himself in all the roles: Richard the Lionheart, Robin of Locksley (better known as Robin Hood, his favourite role), Rowena and Rebecca. He held a water glass to his eye as a telescope to spy out Normans, used a broom handle as a lance, made camp under the kitchen table. When another boy tried to join in, he waved him away.

'Why won't you play with him?' Hannes asked.

Samuel looked at him, calm, face upturned, as if demonstrating that he was paying attention. He let the reproach wash over him and, as soon as Hannes had finished, ran off into the garden. The other boy ducked under the table, took the glass and broom handle and continued the game in his own way.

In the almond tree, branches shook.

A climbing figure disappeared into the treetop.

Hannes, who had followed him, stopped undecided in the yard. Nothing to see but colourless outlines in the dark. He feared that the boy would have a hard time at school. Hannes had enough dealings with children to know how loners like Samuel fared. But how could he lessen what lay in store for his son? What did his constant reprimands achieve – apart from casting him in the role of strict father? Florentine's 'Give it time' was so much more beautiful. Perhaps she was right when she said that a child would eventually rear itself, with the help of neighbours, friends and seasons.

'You Germans risk little for your dead.'

Hannes gave a start. He had not noticed Ovidiu who, clearly surprised at Hannes' new jumpiness, now handed him a glass of wine. First he poured a few drops from each of their glasses onto the ground – in memory of Echo.

'You don't even buy them new shoes.'

In Romanian folklore, everything you ate, drank and bought was an investment in the dead person's final journey.

'In heaven, you can walk barefoot.'

'And if you're headed the opposite way?' Ovidiu asked, a finger pointing downwards.

Hannes laughed and felt a deep affection for this man, who always had another version of the truth to hand.

A gust of wind caressed Hannes' face and throat, caught in his hair, a surprise attack – and then withdrew just as swiftly.

He didn't understand why the wind had a bad reputation, Ovidiu remarked. The wind carried seeds away in search of good soil. For something to grow, all it needed was the touch of the wind. Wasn't that what the church preached?

Hannes did not get as far as seeking an answer. A group had gathered outside the door, Ruth among them. Their too-loud voices told him that something was wrong.

Severin had disappeared.

'But he won't have…' someone ventured.

'No, he won't,' said Hannes.

Ovidiu still went to the cemetery, just in case.

Ruth seemed frozen in her rage. The day's tasks, small and large, had stopped the hours falling into the abyss. But after that day came the next, where less consolation was to be found, and in the week that followed things would pick up where they had left off, the number of visits would dwindle, the small kindnesses, until finally she too would be expected to find her way back to what called itself normality. Life goes on, they said, not seeing how threatening those words sounded. Life went on and so did death; on every single day to come, Echo would not be there.

Hannes would have liked to say to Ruth that it was easier to accept that God's will be done than to accept the facts themselves. That what mattered now was not to understand, but to believe that you were loved all the same. He wished she and Severin would find each other in their grief. The words were there, but it was impossible to speak them; they would come out wrong and be no help to Ruth. The wind rose again, but this time something touched Hannes gently. An owlet moth settled on his forearm. Hannes raised it carefully to eye level. He and Ruth contemplated the moth's wings, a pattern of black waves with a light turquoise playing at its edges.

When Ruth turned away, her expression had changed, and Hannes thought (or perhaps just wished) that this might have been the suggestion of a smile.

A voice rang out from the almond tree. 'He's in the cowshed.'

Another shake of the branches. A leap.

Hannes wanted to show Samuel the moth, but it was gone.

They joined hands and went to the byre. A dim light shone in the dusk. The cows chewed devotedly, hardly any turning their heads to look. Towards the back of the shed, a lamp stood on the floor. Hannes picked it up, set it on a wooden beam. Only then did he see Severin. At first, he could not make sense of this strange contortion, and pulled Samuel to him.

The yearling's eyes were moist, her head inclined a little to one side. She looked surprised. Her light coat, which seemed colourless and dull in daylight, shone like silk.

Severin knelt beside her.
Embracing the heifer who dreamed.

# Leviathan

· · · · ·

Now, right now, without knowing why, she could feel the king's hand in hers. He was smiling. His smile was like the sunrise – heralded by birds long before you saw it. The April day was warm, the birds sang in the trees, they took wing, and King Michael the First smiled.

Memory is a room with wandering doors. Sometimes the shadow of a mountain will strike you, sometimes a word. You might be walking up a hill, carrying a basket of apples, washing your hair, and all at once a door opens. And then one morning you don't want to get out of bed, or to do anything.

Because memory is enough.

Karlina grated potatoes and fried them. She added too much salt. She pounded and deep fried the pork schnitzels. She mixed oil, vinegar and sugar for the salad. Her husband and the boy sat and said a prayer. The meal lasted little more than twenty minutes. The boy asked if he could leave the table. He had the gift of making himself invisible, appearing only for meals. Johann took his newspaper to the arbour, and Karlina cleared the table and washed the dishes.

You spend all morning in the kitchen, she thought, the man eats without a word of thanks, and then has nothing better to do than read the paper and pick his teeth.

Her mother wanted sons and birthed four daughters. Karlina was the second eldest and because they had been hoping for a Karl, she received this name that took effort to flesh out. There were no role models for life as a Karlina. Her Hungarian governess used to call her Károly whenever she was angry. She recalled the rustle of the damask dress, the cool scent of jasmine and peppermint, and the lisp that her governess tried in vain to master when agitated. It gave her a momentary air of helplessness. Then Karlina felt satisfaction: the tongue striking the front teeth was appropriate punishment for twisting her name into that Hungarian masculine.

Her first boyfriend had an English mother and decided to call her Charlie. She liked the sound, really liked it. Even now – though this happened less and less – looking at her reflection with a degree of approval, skin soft from the bath, the lines around her eyes smoothed and grey hair obscured by steam, she would call herself Charlie in her mind, closing her eyes and running her fingertips across her throat as Ernest used to, slowly, lost in the moment, making each touch all the more delicious – something most of the men in her life had not understood. Touching with an aim in mind killed all sensuality. Karlina had had an inkling of it at least once in her life, and for this she was glad.

In this way, fortified by memories, the everyday became bearable for a while. All week it was: Lina, come here a minute. Lina, someone's at the door. Lina, the loft is untidy. Lina, I can't find my things. Sometimes she wished she could be rid of the 'lina' at the end of her name, since that nickname had prevailed – not the spirited Károly or the tender Charlie. How would her life have played out if her mother's dearest wish had been fulfilled? What if the king had shaken hands with a Karl?

No, she only wanted to have shaken hands with the king as a woman. It was one of those moments when being a woman paid off.

Karlina leaned on the door of the summer kitchen. She had put away the dishes, cleaned the stovetop, removed the tablecloth. Johann, meanwhile, had fallen asleep in the arbour. A butterfly took his belly for a hill. He was fatter than a person should be in these times. To harbour a grudge was to swallow poison and expect someone else to die – yet day after day she was irritated with Johann, whose actions and omissions formed a constant undercurrent of annoyance. His silence towards her was final proof that he, too, had mislaid what they had once called love.

How fortunate that Karlina had the gift of directing her thoughts elsewhere. She could believe six impossible things before breakfast. First: Johann would change. Second: for the better. Third: they would print something intelligent in the newspaper for once. Fourth: she would find a cure for varicose veins. Fifth: someone would find a cure for communism. Sixth: one day, the monarchy would be restored.

She, for one, was ready.

Karlina untied her apron, closed up the summer kitchen. No sound reached her from the gardens, or the street, no one strolling, chatting, playing music. No skipping rope hummed through the air, no ball bounced off a wall. The early afternoon silence suddenly felt fathomless. Should she sit in the arbour, stretch out on the chaise longue? Make a start on the ironing?

She decided to check on the boy. He needed a bath before his father arrived. Karlina walked round to the front, up the steps, through the vestibule and into the main house. She closed a cupboard door that always opened by itself, straightened a curtain, called his name. He didn't answer. Cautiously, she opened the door to the living room, but he was neither in the reading chair nor at the table with his schoolbooks. The kitchen, too, was empty. Karlina closed the shutters to keep out the heat. She thought back to the outing that had given her one more opportunity to use her parasol. Life did hold some legitimate pleasures, after all. These included an elegant dressing gown, nut liqueur steeped with cinnamon and coffee beans, and gliding across the fish pond in a rowing boat beneath a parasol – while others dripped with sweat under glaring sun. May every one seek their own salvation.

Karlina had worn an ankle-length floral dress, so out of date that it could be described as timeless. She dressed her grandson carefully, regretting that he was not yet old enough for a hat. She hoped that hats would never fall out of fashion; a hat was the most essential item of clothing for a man. They had taken the bus to the zoo. The boy had shown no delight in the animals; while other children viewed the parrots with curiosity and the lions with awe, his expression grew ever more solemn. When they reached the bears, he asked if they could go. Karlina, also tiring of the odour of fur and dung, suggested a boat ride. She put up the crocheted cream parasol. Patterns of light and shade moved over her shoulders, her dress. The boy trailed a hand in the water and watched the rower. He was interested in everything that moved, horse-drawn carts, tractors, trains, cars, aeroplanes, and had become an excellent bicyclist at an early age, something that she still could not bring herself to attempt.

Karlina went into the 'third room', so called because it had no single purpose, serving as housework room, study or guest room as required. She stepped into the half-dark. The oak table was piled with newspapers and ironing; clothes and towels hung on chairs waiting to be mended. Holes, torn loops, stuck zips – no buttons in this house, except on Johann's shirts (for which she secretly did not forgive him). Karlina made sure of that.

By the window stood a tower of mattresses. It reached almost to the ceiling and came from the time of big parties and numerous guests. Then, the mattresses had been laid out to cover the floor of this room, which had no oak table then, turning it into a dormitory where a dozen people could sleep. Twelve mattresses, with shining, silky slip covers in every hue from poppy red and raspberry pink to corn yellow, lavender and larkspur blue. The sea green one always had to be uppermost. Karlina didn't know why. Nor did she know why the mattresses were still there; it was a long time since they had welcomed guests in such numbers. She had never minded cooking for a dozen, but now felt tired just wondering what to make for herself and Johann in the coming week. Perhaps it was because those earlier meals had lasted more than twenty minutes; no one had retreated wordlessly to the shade of the arbour and people had never ever failed to praise her famous chicken soup or her ciorbă de perișoare.

Karlina studied the floral pattern of the mattress tower and felt a longing for that time. People had lain in this room, enduring all the smells and noises, the fumes, the snoring. She had always opened the double window, even on New Year's Eve. On Easter night, on birthday and carnival nights. On every one of those nights.

She knew exactly where the boy was, of course. She just wanted to be sure she hadn't overlooked him elsewhere. Or perhaps she was reluctant to spoil his pleasure at remaining undiscovered for a while. Karlina climbed onto a stool and felt around on the top mattress.

'What are you doing up there?'

'I'm hiding.'

'I found you.'

'No you didn't. It's a secret place.'

Samuel would know that. Now that no one slept on these mattresses, now that they were nothing but memory piled in a corner, this was the most out-of-the-way place in the house.

She heard a page turn. The boy was still ruining his eyesight with all that reading.

Karlina leaned against the mattresses, her eyes roaming the room without alighting on the edges of the table, the ascending lines of the cupboard or the pattern of the embroidered wall hanging – and listened to Samuel's breathing. It reminded her of her sons' breathing in the evening, at bedtime. Three boys seldom in the mood for sleep. Had that been her revenge on her mother? Three sons with proper names: Hannes, Hermann and Günter.

'Tell me about the Transilvania.'

Samuel looked down from the mattresses. Karlina looked up. The slits of light through the closed shutters reflected in his eyes, aligning with his straight brows. No one could agree on the colour of his eyes. Light brown, people said, but Karlina, who could not decide between goose-grey and cinnamon-brown, was living proof that they lacked imagination.

They looked at one another, Karlina on her stool, her back against the mattress tower, the boy on the sea green mattress, two hand-breadths below the ceiling.

Something was on his mind. He had grown quieter and quieter as the time to leave drew near. Karlina noticed, even though – or possibly because – he was always quiet.

'The Transilvania?'

The boy nodded.

She had told him the story many times. Did he notice the deviations? Did he see what she omitted, what she stressed, what she exaggerated for the sheer pleasure of it? You had to be careful, telling stories. If you drifted from a set course into uncharted waters, other things might surface: longings, fears, truths. They had entered that room with wandering doors and clouded windows where it was a given that nothing, least of all hopes, could be left behind forever.

Karlina expected the capricious, the unpredictable, the contradictory. People told stories in a strangely invariable way, as if they had really happened like that. And yet, Karlina suspected, all stories happened in a hundred possible ways, all equally true and untrue.

Two years before the king shook Karlina's hand, Johann had seduced her under the apple tree in her parents' garden. From the coach house, you could scarcely see the house, the latticed windows, the carved canopy of the veranda, the cast iron weathercock on the gable. It wasn't turning. The grass was September warm and the trees lay in darkness, with just a little moon-silver in their branches. Johann's kisses were urgent, he pressed himself against her, uttered words of love, kissed every inch of bare skin. Something scurried away (her will, her good sense?), and another force took over. This she could not fight, and the longer she tried, the more unlikely it became to find any way back. Eventually the lawn rug, the weathercock and apple lights all vanished, and in their place came sensations that freed her from wishing, from thinking, wanting, longing, and yet entrenched themselves as longing and desire forever.

Karlina withheld this scene, of course, although it was where the Transilvania business began. This act was a quiet prelude, so to speak, played just for her in the chamber of memory.

Whether you start with apple or sycamore, this story still belongs to you, thought Karlina, and it remained astonishing that both Johann and the king could be held in the same space.

For her grandson, Karlina would begin the tale with her family's summer holiday in Mamaia. With the packed trunks, the excitement that reigned before departure, the train compartment with its red curtains and uniformed waiter. The doctor had counselled her against the trip; her pregnancy was already advanced, but she had flung his warning to the winds (never imagining that the winds would bring it back to her). The longing for the seagull house was too great.

She said nothing on the journey when she first felt a dragging pain, and she said nothing when Johann wrote that he couldn't follow on. In all honesty, the prospect of a few weeks to herself before becoming a mother was a relief. She sat on the terrace and watched the sun rise over the sea. She went walking on the beach with Emma, Marie or Auguste, but mostly with Emma, her eldest sister, who was the best at adapting to her new tempo. She breakfasted in the garden beneath the sycamore. The lacy, five-pointed leaves rustled, light veins showed through leaf skins, and a line of shade advanced very slowly across the lawn. The housekeeper served coffee; her father read the newspaper. Her mother and sisters might still be in bed, in the bathroom, or at the breakfast table (though rarely all together). Karlina was always the first to wake. She crossed the lawn barefoot in her dressing gown and searched inside herself for a life that might possibly suit her better than these days.

With her belly, she could no longer swim, or walk for long or bathe in the sun, but the salty taste of the air was the same, as was hot sand under the soles of her feet, and the surprising chill of the water, which always made her retreat a few steps and then, enjoying her small hesitation, venture on into the surf, wave after wave.

Karlina's parents may not have been happy with this son-in-law (they had been hoping for one of the young heirs from their circle of friends), but apple-tree nights with a weathercock who slept through his watch could not be undone. The facts had to be accepted. A growing belly was one such fact.

Karlina's family ran the most successful wool-scouring plant in Transylvania. For years, her father had experimented with various processes for cleaning dung, grass and sweat from fleeces. A delicate business. Wool would not tolerate extreme fluctuations in temperature, and excessive scrubbing produced felts, which were to be avoided. The cleaning process needed to retain some of the lanolin. Karlina's father had lost a finger to his first machine, two more to his second. It was an art, finding the right sequences, settings, speeds; sheep's coats were shaped by altitude and temperature, how the animals were fed and treated, and their tendency to felt varied (as was true of humans, too). Bohemian mestizo wool required different settings to Hungarian Racka or Turkish Karaman.

Karlina's mother asked her husband to stop experimenting, since the emerging pattern suggested he would lose three fingers next time. The machine he eventually developed and patented still bore similarities to the Leviathan, which had been in use since eighteen sixty-three. It consisted of a scouring tank, in which the pre-sorted wool was immersed by a rotating drum and swirled around while a fork stabbed rhythmically into the wool. But whereas the Leviathan had a rake to lift out the wool and transport it to a second tank, and then a third, possibly a fourth, the machine developed by Karlina's father confined the whole process to a single tank. The water was expelled and refilled until the wool was clean and could be air-dried. This space-saving system allowed a lot of small businesses to start operating, which mattered in a country with more sheep than people.

Sales of the 'All-in-one tank', and income from a factory in Heltau that specialised in cleaning silky lambswool, saw the family prosper. In possession of his seven remaining fingers, Karlina's father had bought a villa in the upper town, the seagull house on the Black Sea coast, and a mountain chalet on the Hohe Rinne. Every time they saw a flock of sheep, his daughters experienced a vague sense of wellbeing, a mixture of sympathy, melancholy and gratitude. For Karlina, this feeling had extended over the years to the sight of clouds. Whenever she felt discouraged, a drifting cloud formation was enough to console her.

Who would dispute the similarities?

Karlina became aware of a touch, and raised her head. The boy had shifted to the edge of the mattress, and his hand was on her shoulder.

'So, sheep. Go on,' he said, and waited until the sheep in her memory had evaporated, one by one, like clouds dispersing in a summer sky.

At the end of June, three weeks after their arrival, a passenger ship called the Transilvania docked in Constanța. As Karlina's father had business dealings with the Burmeister & Wain shipyard in Denmark – the carpets on the Selandia, the world's first motorised sea-going vessel, were woven from Heltau lambswool – the family was allowed to visit the ship between voyages. It could hold four hundred and twelve passengers, crossing the Black Sea, the Mediterranean and the Red Sea.

The waves were high; the radio issued a storm warning.

'Vine furtuna,' the storm is coming, said the fishermen.

Nevertheless, the sisters pressed for a tour. After all, the ship was moored in the harbour, it couldn't capsize, and no better entertainment for a wet-weather day could be imagined. Only Karlina's mother stayed at home, feeling unwell, or claiming to, in the hope of some peace.

First, they visited the upper deck, which afforded a view of Romania's only seaport, and the oldest part of the town on the promontory. You could see the minaret of the Piaţa Ovidiu mosque, built in nineteen ten at the behest of King Carol the First (Karlina knew her royal history), and the casino on the cliffs built the same year. At the end of the nineteenth century, the German community had also been endowed with a church and a school – the only Protestant school in the whole of Dobruja – but they weren't visible from here. To the other side of the handrail lay the harbour wall, then open sea. Marie leaned playfully over the rail and whistled a tune until the bearded Lipovan, introduced to them as Ivan, barked at her to stop.

Did she not know that whistling was forbidden on a ship. Whistling would call something up, at worst a storm, and no one wanted a Jonah on board.

Behind the coarse-meshed safety net which the captain termed a corpse-catcher – to general surprise, since at the moment of going overboard one was hopefully very much alive – loomed a triangular wall of grey-black cloud. This pyramid had already swallowed the sun, and a glistening halo shone around its peak as the procession went down into the belly of the ship.

While the sisters expressed interest in the cabins and the dining room, asking about crockery and crystalware, their father wanted to see the engine room first, and got his way. The captain went ahead, and Ivan told them about the engines expertly and at great length. Then the men strayed into political waters. According to Karlina's father, the Germans were on the point of starting another war.

The air was stuffy, the light from the lamps glaring. The gentle rocking motion gradually became a powerful swaying, which at first Karlina put down to the exceptional clarity her senses always developed at the seaside. She held on and softened her knees to ride out the bucking and bobbing. Auguste felt queasy and reeled off to find a lavatory. Marie followed not long after, and Emma, too, grew pale, but stayed. Karlina lost her sense of time and space. It was not the swaying that worried her, nor the absence of daylight, but the metallic clanks, booms and creaks. The pipes wailed, the floor groaned, the ship hummed and rumbled, and at first Karlina hardly noticed an answering rumble low down in her belly – then she began to feel more intensely the pains that had been with her all day, coming and going at regular intervals. A hot sensation, a stabbing pain, and she heard and felt nothing more.

She found herself in a cabin, the captain on one side of the bed, Ivan on the other, with Emma at the foot. The flood surged against the cabin wall, and a lamp swung to and fro above the bed. Karlina felt panic rising, then humiliation.

'Do not get up,' said the captain.

'But I want to…'

'You father is fetching a doctor. And until he gets here, I ask that you breathe deep into your belly.'

Karlina swallowed her objection. Such nonsense. Breathe calmly! A fierce pain gnawed at her guts, sending out waves through her whole body; her lower back was breaking apart. She turned aside and vomited. Shortly thereafter she emptied her bladder and bowels. Emma helped her with the chamber pot. Karlina's shame was gone now, there was nothing but the inescapable reality of this pain. The ship's clattering, roaring and careening was hers, too; it was a great, all-embracing physical sensation. *She* was the ship, with the rain hammering down and the waves whipping and the storm shaking her, and she was also the wind, the waves, the rain, until eventually something that had been resting on the seabed was unleashed and plunged everything into chaos. A wave lifted the ship, somewhere something was ripped from its anchor, a high, buzzing tone broke away from the upper deck, sank into the hold and continued along the passageways as a meandering echo. Crockery smashed, objects fell and rolled across the floor, a tidal wave crashed against the porthole, darkening the cabin, and Karlina screamed.

By the time her drenched father boarded the Transilvania with a doctor, his first grandchild had arrived. They'd had to wait to come aboard; a wave had breached the harbour wall and reduced the gangway to its constituent parts. His too-loud greeting from the threshold reflected the sight that met him. Objects on the floor, a rumpled bed, excrement and vomit, his daughter drenched in sweat, the baby smeared with blood and engine oil.

Hannes had been born in cabin one hundred and seventy-seven, first-class accommodation with a porthole that once more looked onto a calm waterline. The captain had cut the umbilical cord, and when the baby did not cry, Ivan had turned him upside down and given him several hard slaps on the bottom with oil-covered hands, saying something in Russian that sounded like an invocation. Auguste and Marie had not reappeared. They were found in a cabin on a higher deck, where they had locked themselves in. Emma wrapped the child in a pillowcase and laid him on Karlina's chest.

The ship groaned a lullaby, the wind gently combed the waves and when a few hours later Karlina was stretchered onto the upper deck, a soft rain wetted her face.

Karlina was convinced that the boy was still hiding on the mattresses when Hannes arrived.

'Leave him,' she said. 'He'll reappear when it's time for supper.'

While Hannes went into the wine cellar with Johann, she prepared the pancake filling. She stirred urda, chopped dill, combined the two, and as she was about to pour the first ladle of batter into the pan, a sound detached itself from her memory. The radio, a neighbour calling over the wall, a pigeon's coo – these had not drowned out the opening and closing of the front gate. Karlina had not given it a thought.

Now the noise sounded like a warning.

Karlina turned off the stove and went with sudden haste into the third room, pushed the stool up to the mattresses and felt for a leg, a hand, a head. Then she climbed onto a chair to see better. The sea green mattress was empty but for book, pencil and blanket. Karlina shook out the blanket, as if the boy might yet surface.

'He isn't here?'

Hannes' question was more of a statement.

Karlina, still on the chair, shook her head.

He held out his hand and she stepped down, out of breath, as if she had climbed a mountain.

Karlina searched the house and garden, Johann checked with the neighbours, Hannes scoured the playground and ran all the way to the park. With Johann's help, Karlina pulled down every one of the twelve mattresses. The boy had to be here, somewhere between poppy red, corn yellow and lavender blue, there was no other option.

Then a thought came to her.

'Where are you going?' asked Hannes.

Karlina avoided his gaze, unequal to the worry it held.

'I was telling him about the Black Sea.'

'Then we mustn't lose any time.'

Johann stayed at home in case the boy reappeared. Hannes wanted to cycle. Karlina refused to sit on the pannier rack ('If I get on a bicycle, I shall die,' she said), until Hannes threatened to go without her.

When the woman at the ticket counter told them that the only train to the Black Sea had left at seven o'clock that morning, Karlina's legs gave way with relief. She sat down on a bench. She was quite stiff from the ride, during which she had understood for the first time why the neighbourhood around the station was known as 'The other side'.

A boy huddled in the luggage net of a train compartment: this image had taken hold of her, ignoring the fact that Samuel was far too big for that now. In the past, she thought – and that word hurt because the future was so uncertain – when she'd collected him from the Banat in the school holidays, he had never wanted to sit on the seats. They usually took the Orient Express, which linked Vienna to Bucharest and stopped in Arad around midnight. Karlina would spread out her coat in the luggage net, and Samuel would curl up in it, listening to the rhythm of the rail joints on the wheels, the chat in the compartment, while outside the train windows, fields flew by, telephone masts rising like upturned pitchforks. He usually fell asleep before they reached Deva.

'And now?'

'We keep looking,' said Hannes.

They asked on the station forecourt if anyone had seen a boy with wavy, ash-blond hair, straight eyebrows (they could not agree on eye colour, so this was not mentioned), small ears, gangly, about this tall – Karlina's hand to her neck, Hannes' to his chest. They asked signalmen, carters, taxi drivers, passengers. Samuel, or so it appeared, had not come here. Then a purligar – one of the homeless men who slept on the station concourse – said something.

Karlina took a step back. She looked mistrustfully at the unshaven man, his torn jacket and trousers.

'I saw a boy like that. A farmer took him off towards Heltau. At any rate, he got up on a hay wagon.'

The man held out his open hand.

'So my memory's just as good next time.'

Hannes gave him a few coins. They left the bicycle there and took a taxi to Heltau. When they arrived, the Fogarasch Mountains were already imprinted on the evening sky like a faded ink drawing, grey on dark blue.

Hannes said they should split up. He would search the fields while Karlina called on the pastor. Someone might have seen Samuel. Karlina objected: she knew the fields better; Hannes should try his colleague. Since they could not agree, they continued to search together.

Karlina asked why Samuel didn't want to go to school.

'No one wants to go back to school after the summer holidays.'

Karlina was not content with this answer.

School was an utterly absurd system for preparing children for life, said Hannes. The way they had to sit like soldiers at desks all morning following an arbitrary rhythm of lessons. Curiosity, inquiring minds, everything that came naturally to children was driven out of them. Making mistakes, finding your strengths, learning who you wanted to be, outside of established norms – none of this was important at school. It was a rigid, totalitarian system which, like all systems, at some point began to work against people, not for them.

'What would you have instead?' asked Karlina.

'The courage to try something new: get rid of the desks and the classical subjects, and dismiss all those who have no ideas beyond giving out essays and punishments.'

That to Karlina did not seem very realistic.

Utopias were not meant to be realised, but to point the way, Hannes argued. If they clung to this nonsensical, unreformable school system, society would never pursue anything beyond its own advantage. A few were commended; the majority vanished in the crowd. And someone like Samuel would suffer from the first school year to the last.

'Florentine should take better care of the boy,' Karlina said.

'It's not her fault,' said Hannes. 'He's a loner.'

'There is a place for everyone. For loners, dreamers…'

'If anyone knows that, it's you.'

They had reached the last houses of Heltau.

Although Karlina knew what was coming, the sight was still a blow.

Derelict buildings behind the iron gates, weeds on the roofs. Someone was collecting discarded tyres on the forecourt. The main entrance to the wool-scouring plant was boarded up. A side door opened and a man crossed the forecourt; light-coloured strands of wool had settled on his suit. He raised a hand in greeting to the gatekeeper – his right hand, with its three remaining fingers. Karlina saw balls of downy wool rolling over the floor of the plant and felt something like happiness at the memory.

A time had come when her mother was glad not to have sons. And then a time when it didn't matter what you had. It was a miracle that, out of the void facing the family when their property was seized, something had come that could once more be called life.

Hannes asked if they should check the factory grounds.

Karlina shook her head and kept walking.

The meadows were mown, the mountains dull as dark glass. The wind teased straw from the haystacks, early leaves from alders and robinias.

Hannes turned up the collar of his jacket.

'Are there sheep somewhere here?' Karlina asked – and then she saw it, too. Starlings taking wing, a pulsating fingerprint in the air, and beyond them a flock, scattered over the hills between Heltau and Michelsberg.

They ran, until Karlina got a stitch.

An old woman was not up to such adventures, she said, stopping by an alder.

What if Hannes didn't find the boy? If they were on the wrong track? Where else could they search? What else had she told Samuel? Karlina looked over fields, mountains, the silhouette of the town, until they gradually arranged themselves into a panorama she could recognise.

How far away everything was.

Or was she far away from everything?

You could yearn for what was lost, and for what had not come to pass. You could long to find something, and sometimes also to lose something – and there was always something to reproach yourself with, thought Karlina. Her mind turned to apple tree, to sycamore and seagull house. To the small flat they had been assigned after the war to house five of them somehow. Emma's death, the loss of her parents. The years in the button factory, Johann's silence. Karlina thought of her sons and the marriages they had made, taking them away from her; Florentine in particular was a daughter-in-law she could not fathom. She had advised Hannes against the match, had even hidden his shoes one evening in the hope of preventing a rendezvous. To no avail.

Perhaps it would be better not to have the early, happy memories. Perhaps, without them, life would be unbearable.

When one large and one small shadow detached themselves from the flock of sheep, when the shadows grew, acquiring arms and legs, faces, when Karlina took a few steps forward, then started running, she wished for the boy's life to go in the opposite direction.

That everything to come would be better than what had been.

'I'm sorry,' said Samuel.

Karlina pressed him to her. Hannes was pale, but smiling. They walked across the field, Karlina taking one of the boy's hands, Hannes the other. A neighbour of the pastor's gave them a ride back to Hermannstadt on his cart.

'I want to be a shepherd,' said Samuel as they rode on the cart.

'You can be anything you want,' Karlina told him.

'Just not a fishmonger,' said Hannes. 'Your mother wouldn't like that.'

A person in my position has no biography in the real sense, King Michael is reported to have said.

He reigned for a short while as a five-year-old, was replaced by his father Carol the Second, and took the throne again in nineteen-forty. He resisted the sovietisation of Romania, and the deportation of the German population for forced labour, was made to leave the country and, as far as Karlina knew, he was keeping his head above water in Switzerland as a poultry farmer and test pilot. Every Christmas, he appealed to the Romanian people on Radio Free Europe.

He appealed to her.

That night, Karlina could not sleep. Johann lay beside her, and Samuel and Johannes slept in the next room, on the corn yellow and sea green mattresses. It had been nearly midnight when the pancakes were dished up. Soft cheese filling for the adults, sugar and ground nuts for the boy. The bicycle was either at the station or long gone. She got up, pulled on her dressing gown, poured herself nut liqueur in the kitchen and sipped it, leaning on the window seat.

What has happened in the past makes a claim on you, Karlina thought, closing her eyes. The birds took flight, the morning sun shone on Peleş palace, and the king's smile was just a chimera, though it had lasted all this time. The light preserved it, the warmth of that day, the scent of firs and chestnut trees. Karlina had been young, King Michael was young too, and even more handsome than in his photographs. Karlina ate corn on the cob with salt, so much salt that it burned her lips. A man led a bear on a leash. Dogs barked. A crown was emblazoned on the numberplate of the limousine beside her father's delivery lorry. The statues in front of the palace were covered in moss. One figure held a jug at waist height, the jug seeming to tip without her noticing the water pouring out, a wave captured forever, just as Karlina was forever captured in this moment. Lips numb with salt, her hand enveloped in the hand of the king.

Once his majesty had left, they rested in a meadow in the shade, a spring meadow with dandelions and baby's breath.

The king was gone and yet not gone, because already, Karlina had set out to invent him.

# Wind wanderer

· · · · ·

The tin bath was too small now. This year, her knees stuck out from the water like small islands. The well water had grown warm over the day. She had skimmed off the dead flies, knocked the sand from her feet, hung her clothes over a chair missing one leg. Climbing in, she had sunk into the water until her chin touched the surface. Bent her legs and then, seeing that this wouldn't work, stretched them along the sides of the bath. She wiggled her toes. If sadness dwelled in her breast, then jollity lived in her toes. Everything had its fixed place in the body, thought Stana, and she was working on filling out the whole of this map.

She liked her underwater body. Her thighs felt smooth, her breasts firm. Her hair was soft, scratches and impurities vanished. She ran a hand over her stomach, up her ribs to her throat, closed her eyes. Swallows chattered in the silver poplar – or was it just one? One swallow could sound like two, in constant dialogue with itself.

No one could see Stana. The walls between her and the neighbouring houses were high; only one small attic window in her own house overlooked the vegetable garden. And there was no one in the loft, except in autumn, when they laid out nuts, or when her mother was looking for something put away after the move that was needed in the household: a stuttering coffee grinder; a clock that ticked too loudly; hopelessly knotted shoelaces.

Stana had been waiting for the moment her father left the house. Some fathers went to work in the morning and didn't come home until evening. Others, the majority in fact, worked their own land. She wished hers was the first kind. A father who was gone all day, who couldn't just appear when she and her mother were peeling potatoes and laughing (about him, or so he assumed), who couldn't just stand in the doorway when she was lying on her bed, reading (laziness, he called that). Perhaps that was the most dislikeable thing about him: the constant appraisal with conclusions that seldom flattered her or her mother. Every single thing that happened was about him. If someone looked at the floor, they had a bad conscience; if someone looked him in the eye, it was a provocation; if people whispered in his presence, they were going behind his back; if someone was silent, they simply didn't like him. His life was suspicion and unforgiveness, punctuated with moments of calm or something like it – indifference, perhaps. She could feel his presence beside the tin tub, his eyes on her light, thin body, blurred beneath the surface of the water. Was that a noise? Stana gave a start. Water sloshed over.

Tree shadows lengthened across the yard. A mouse ran over the grass and disappeared into the shed. The vegetable bed lay in the sun, peppers ripening beside tomatoes, green beans beside courgettes. Watermelons lay on the earth, so large they had to be rolled into the house. Stana would fill the watering can with the bathwater and, as soon as the shadow of the house next door reached the yard, she would water the beds, vinete and tomatoes only from below, knock on the watermelons and listen for the bright, hollow sound that would tell her they were ripe. Where they lived before, there had only been a balcony, and here the garden had become a new chore for Stana, one she liked much better than being in charge of the laundry.

But before setting about her evening routine, she took a breath, pulled in her legs and went under. Underwater, she opened her eyes. All she saw was unobstructed blue, and all she heard the sound of the tub, an echo of her movements. Then a face appeared above the water. Ash blond, wavy hair, barley-coloured eyes and straight eyebrows.

The shame was still burning in her stomach when she went to bed. She had not spoken at supper, responding neither to her mother's questioning glances nor to her father's remarks which, as usual, expressed degrees of reproach. She had watered the beds, tipped the tub to pour out the rest. Its high, metallic clang sounded like her anger.

It had taken all her self-control to sit up in the tub and cover what had been exposed moments before. At first, she couldn't speak. Nor could he. But she could see how uncertain he too was, surprised, embarrassed and on the point of leaving without a word.

'Turn around,' said Stana.

He turned around.

She rose from the tub, wrapped herself in a towel and sat on the three-legged chair, regretting it at once because of course it wobbled – making it even more of an effort to cling to the remains of her self-assurance.

A caterpillar crawled along the edge of the tub. Its green body seemed translucent. A moth fought the water, trying not to drown.

'What are you doing here?'

Samuel turned back to her. His eyes fixed on her face. Not on the towel she was clutching to her, not on her legs, where droplets of water shimmered, not on the rivulets running from the hair plastered to her neck.

'Sana, I just wanted…'

The depth of his embarrassment was clear. The situation demanded more of him than of her, though she was the one who had lain naked on the bottom of the tub and now wobbled on a three-legged chair summoning all the dignity she could find.

'Let's talk another time,' she said, rescuing the moth with a cupped hand.

He strode off across the yard at a pace that still passed for walking and not running, as if he had just been waiting for her to finally release him.

Even in bed, Stana could think of little else.

Her room faced the street. From time to time, footsteps passed by. A car's headlights scanned the walls, then it was dark again. What had he imagined? He must have seen her clothes on the chair. Had he assumed she was wearing a bathing suit, like she did down by the Marosch? Did he mean to give her a fright? He had not moved, had looked at her like some strange thing – and yet no one's face was more familiar to her than his. There had never been a time without Samuel. They had spent evenings under the kitchen table while their parents played cards. Built a den of blankets and cushions in the living room and tried to convince the adults it was their home now: food could be passed in through the opening, more toys would have to be provided, personal hygiene was to be neglected.

She had ridden donkeys with Samuel and herded sheep. They didn't shy away from risk, making faces though people said your face would stay like that forever if the church clock struck, drinking water before a meal though frogs would grow in your stomach if you drank too much. Samuel had cured her fear of water, after a course in Arad where the teacher had pushed her into the pool with a poorly inflated rubber ring and said: Now swim! That was just how it was done, he told Stana's mother, who collected a weeping child from every lesson. If she wanted to raise a coward, she was welcome to take her daughter off the course. And because Stana's parents could not swim and no one, least of all her father, wanted to raise a coward, Stana was not taken off the course.

The water will hold you, Samuel said, you just have to make yourself light.

As light as a parachute from a dandelion clock?

As light as a sycamore propeller?

Yes.

Stana learned from the wind wanderers. She learned not to fight the water, and not to fight her father. Not at every opportunity, not always. Samuel had taught her when to avoid his gaze and when to hold it. You don't look a rearing horse in the eye, but you do look at an aggressive dog – calmly, without staring. He must see your strength, but not feel threatened.

It became her mission to tell the horse days from the dog days. Sometimes it went awry, sometimes there was no way of anticipating what had angered her father. Once, he sent her outside in winter because the washing had been hung the wrong way up. There had been a frost, and his undergarments, shirts and trousers were frozen. A casual gesture had shown her what would happen if the washing broke, and it took her almost an hour – working carefully, stiff-fingered – to take down and rehang every single piece.

Trouser waists down, shirt collars too, or it looked like a person was hanging on the line, he said. Like he himself was hanging there.

Some things only her mother knew about, but even when Stana had a swollen eye or a split lip, everyone pretended nothing was split or swollen. Doors got in the way, objects became things you walked into. Fickle, unreliable furniture had a life of its own, leaping out at Stana so fast she couldn't avoid it. Sometimes she walked into a doorframe deliberately, in front of everyone. She was pretty good at that.

But she could not deceive Samuel. Under his gaze, things solidified. He could capture them or make them disappear, depending. In summer, Samuel's eyes were the colour of ripe barley; in autumn they turned amber, a comparison Stana first made when her mother gave her an amber pendant for her fourteenth birthday.

When she thought about where Samuel lived in her body, she realised that he was everywhere. She felt him in her fingertips, in the strength of her shoulders. He had taken over a large space in the middle of her chest, and sent a light feeling into her stomach, like birds taking flight. Lately there was a connection between the region of her heart and her belly, a hot, exuberant, very unsettling feeling. She pulled the covers up under her chin. Without knowing it, Samuel had occupied the map of her body; one thing she was grateful for that evening was that this atlas was invisible.

Sunday came. Like many Slovakians, Stana's family attended the Protestant church. Her mother felt a need for it and her father wanted to spy on people.

Konstanty Novac was out of sorts. It had been a short night; he had been dragged out of bed at eleven in the evening. Stana kept quiet. She could move noiselessly along the hallway, busy herself in the kitchen making almost no sound, as if all the doors, windows and other objects that loved to play tricks on her had suddenly disappeared, with their repertoire of rustles, echoes, bangs and crashes. A world made of cotton wool, white, insulating, invisible cotton wool, always to hand, right there in your pocket.

Malva, her mother, knew no cotton wool.

She was washing her hair, thoroughly, had been dawdling in the bathroom for half an hour, as if the bathroom was not shared with others, as if there was no fixed time to leave the house, as dressed and washed and combed as possible. There was no response when Stana's father demanded that she open the door, or when he rattled it. What was going to happen was clear to all three. Rage rose in Stana, not at her father, but at her mother, who could not resist provoking him.

The bathroom door opened. Stana's mother walked out, freshly washed hair falling in curls on her shoulders (taming these curls took time, thought Stana, surely he must see that), lips red, in her grey, pleated Sunday dress. She looked resolute and yet absent, like someone who has rehearsed a role. He hit her in the face. She stumbled, put a hand to her mouth, went to the window, took a mirror and touched up her lipstick. The bathroom door slammed behind Konstanty. They heard gurgling, the splashing of the tap, the toilet flush. Stana could see in her mother's hand mirror that her eyes were filled with tears. But none rolled down her cheeks. Malva's eyes were like the rain barrel in the garden, full to the brim but never running over, even after heavy rain. The water's surface domed, elastic.

She would turn around, ask Stana if she was ready, in a voice aiming at her but missing by a hair's breadth. He would come out of the bathroom, have her tie his tie. Too much aftershave, too much bonhomie. And then, handbag in the crook of one arm, she would slip the other through his, and as they entered the church he would take her hand, like every Sunday. Only someone looking very closely at Stana's mother, which no one did, would see that one of her cheeks was redder than the other.

Perhaps, possibly, Florentine.

The service began with the introit, the kyrie and the hymn of praise. Then came readings and the sermon. Stana looked to the front row. Samuel was sitting round-shouldered in the pew,

Florentine looking up at the church's ceiling of stars, which assured her of God's presence more than any words from the Bible. The liturgy should not be held seated in this church, but lying down, why else did the miracle of this starry sky exist. Florentine dared to say such things, even to her husband, who now stood in his cassock in the pulpit.

Stana loved Samuel's mother. Her scent of roses, which came from the dried rose petals she placed in her underwear drawer (lemon balm in Samuel's, lavender in her husband's). Her way of speaking, and of not speaking, a quietness that Samuel shared, the ability to say the essential things with her eyes. She liked how Florentine ran her household. Certain things could be left, the dust and crockery, while others were strictly regulated, the garden, the laundry. When Florentine ironed, she would step into the yard and whirl the little iron ship in the air with an outstretched arm to enliven the embers – fearing that indoors, a spark might fly onto something. Before leaving the kitchen she would check several times that the stove was off, and the candles out, though they had never been lit. She boiled her laundry in the garden and in winter laid the rugs out on the snow to clean themselves, while others beat them with a carpet beater.

When Stana and Samuel were children, Florentine had bathed them in the washtub in the garden, and then dried them as carefully as if they were made of glass. Stana had lifted first one foot and then the other onto the rim of the tub, and Florentine had dried each toe, each space between, five toes, four spaces between, with an attention, affection and devotion revealing the magnitude of her love. Even now when Stana dried herself thoughtlessly, with no special tenderness, feet last and hastily, the memory flashed through her: ten toes, eight spaces between, and leaving the bath, she felt that she owed herself something.

'Is it worth the fight?'

Samuel's father paused in his sermon, his eyes roaming over the congregation and seeming to pause longer on the pew where Stana's family sat. Something had shifted while she sat lost in thought, something had changed.

'All the religious leaders supported the king's plan to fight the Babylonians. We will not be defeated, they said, God is with us. Only one prophet in Jerusalem, Jeremiah, warned against the war and drew hatred from the powerful and the priests, who eventually managed to throw him in jail. The king visited him there. Is there a word from the Lord? he asked. He was expecting counsel, a comforting Word of God. But Jeremiah said: You will fall into the hands of the king of Babel. God will not save you.'

The pastor closed the Bible, slowly, as if weighing up his next words.

'Jeremiah did not fear the king's punishment. He was prepared to tell the truth.'

Samuel's back was now straight and Florentine was not looking at the stars. Stana's mother stiffened. It was very still, no one turning the pages of the hymn book, whispering, coughing. With every breath, the silence expanded through the church.

'God is not only a God of the near, but of the far, and dishonesty and hypocrisy does not escape Him. He can turn away from His people. If you do not believe, you will not last, that is what Jeremiah has to tell us today.'

Samuel's father spread his arms. The organ started up. Voices were raised in song. And the singing was loud, louder than the hymns before.

After the closing benediction, he bade the parishioners farewell at the church door. Stana saw that only her mother shook hands with the pastor. Now the whist evenings would be paused once more. And for a time, without openly avoiding her father, people would keep a safe distance. For days, weeks, Malva would meet Florentine in secret, until enough time had passed and they could visit each other again.

Florentine and Samuel waited under a chestnut tree. Stana walked over to them with her mother, feeling as if she was still keeping her balance on the chair with the missing leg.

Florentine folded Stana in her arms by way of greeting.

The women talked about something or other.

Stana looked fixedly past everyone until it was time to go.

'King's children?' Samuel whispered. 'Tomorrow afternoon.'

Stana nodded.

No one but him would have seen it.

The wheat fields had been harvested, the maize still stood. The plain stretched as far as the eye could see. The sky laid claim to a vast space, with no mountains or forests to raise an objection. The Marosch snaked like a vein through the flat land.

Stana walked across the maize field. It was forbidden, but who took any notice of that? On a hot day, there was nothing like the cool air locked between the long rows of plants. Half the distance to the river could be covered this way. In the shade, said the adults. Under capitals of cucuruz, said Stana and Samuel, who had read the word in an architectural guide.

Samuel waited at a distance from the shallow bank where everyone bathed. Old ladies in bathing robes that ballooned as they crouched down in the water. Farmers washing their horses, shepherds the woollen coats of their sheep. Stana and Samuel had their own place, further upstream by a willow. You could swing into the river on those branches and lie under them, as if behind a curtain. A place where the water was deep, but the current not too strong. On the far side of the river stood another willow, like a reflection. The two trees were called the king's children. They had always had that name.

Samuel lay on his back, arms behind his head. He had grown tall, his arms powerful. Shadows bordered his profile, torso, hips, his outstretched legs – he lay completely still, and yet something seemed to be quivering. Stana sat down beside him.

Slowly, his eyes opened. There was no recognition in them, nothing to read there, no emotion that said he had seen her. Stana, however, saw various things. Obvious things. She saw he had been in the water. He must have been here a while, because the droplets on his skin were small and would soon have vanished. She saw the raised lines of his mouth, the light, downy hair on his cheeks. She saw that his eyes were dark that summer, darker than usual, with a gravity and presence she had never seen in anyone else. She resolved to be more careful from now on (as though revelations could be prevented), and she saw too that he was being more careful than usual.

It was only when Stana deliberately broke the silence that she realised they had been looking into each other's eyes, as if behind them lay tiny escapes to be discovered. Not holding each other's gaze. Falling into it.

'You've been quarrelling with Valentin again.'

She had heard it from a friend in Samuel's class. A teacher was ill, and two classes had been put together, Samuel's and that of Oswald, known as Oz. Samuel's friend had to stand in the corner for two periods because he'd forgotten his German book. If you were in the corner, you were not allowed to eat or drink, or go to the toilet. In the long break, Samuel asked the teacher to lift the punishment.

Why should he do that, said Herr Valentin.

Because it was not proportionate, Samuel replied.

This resulted in Oz sitting down, and Samuel standing in the corner for the rest of the morning.

'He's a sadist.'

Samuel had picked up this word somewhere, using it only for his class teacher.

'Valentin is frustrated because he's a village schoolteacher, having to teach children who will only ever mind cows and till fields,' she said.

'That's not what you're going to do,' said Samuel.

Stana blushed.

In the water, in the middle of the river, self-reproach set in. She had said something for the sake of it. Because the line between her and Samuel was beginning to dissolve. She had started talking about school and quashed what was between them – something that never needed anything to sustain it, no words or assurances, and above all was without shame. How long had they looked at one another? What happened if you yielded, stopped holding back?

Language could be no more than a run-up to the jump.

Stana swam upstream realising that something had gone for good. Nothing would bring it back. Life had shifted with a great swing, pivoting around the bathtub. She turned on her own axis and let herself float. Samuel was waiting level with the king's children. She drifted towards him, considered changing direction, made a half-hearted attempt, gave in, and knew she was coming closer, the water carrying her into his arms. The gentle pressure of his hand on her back was enough to stop her. She made herself light, tilted her head back. Sycamore seed, she thought, dandelion. Samuel turned, and the movement raised her arms. Her face softened, the tension fell away. Was it a wave that pressed her to him, so close that her head touched his chest – a sensation that moved hotly through her – or the memory that he had seen her from this angle yesterday, without a bathing suit? Her stomach muscles clenched, and a powerful swimming stroke put some distance between them. She didn't look at him as she climbed onto the bank, shook the blanket and lay down on her front, to hide her face. She heard him lying down next to her, heard the willow branches pawing at the ground, felt how close he was, so close that his forearm touched hers. The spot grew warm, pulsed, her heart dropped from her chest and was beating there now. The water whispered in her ears; an ant strayed onto her hand.

Stana took shallow breaths into the crook of her arm. Sadness filled the place where her heart had once been, though she didn't know why, and didn't dare move.

Contrary to Stana's expectation, the next whist evening took place as usual.

Samuel's parents invited them.

'I'm not going,' said Stana's father.

'You are going, I am, we all are,' said Stana's mother.

Konstanty Novac had split himself into two. Once he must have been that man who fell in love with her mother, who wanted to become a father. Who dripped páli schnapps into her mouth and Samuel's when they were babies, to stop them getting worms, to help them sleep and not disrupt the card games. Who, when they were children, whipped up raw egg yolk and sugar for them, who took them to the market in Arad, where they sold caged doves, frogs' legs, moonwort and gold jewellery. That man had been mislaid, as you mislay something you seldom use. It's swallowed by the house, and by the years in which you make no use of it, and one day you remember and want it back, but it's gone.

It was possible, as Stana and Malva knew, to spend years in the company of a memory, with the image of a person who was long gone.

Sometimes when Konstanty was drunk, needed comfort, was perhaps seeking forgiveness, words slipped out of him, monstrous words that frightened Stana.

'The Party doesn't make mistakes,' he said, when Stana's mother came to the defence of a man from the pig farm who had been arrested. 'Give him up.'

Malva said nothing. The man was given up.

Then for weeks people turned their faces away when they passed Konstanty, or looked at him as if they had something to prove. Few had the knack of telling horse days from dog days. No objections were voiced, no argument started, but no one was honest, either. The regular gifts of food still continued to arrive. There was always butter on their table, milk, sausages. Stana never had to go out early to queue, like other young people, for a kilo of flour, sugar or oil, to be hoarded and exchanged for something else. She could hand over the kilo of rose hips that every pupil had to bring in after the summer holidays, without knowing who'd supplied it. She was not punished when she forgot her homework or her test score was lower than expected, as were Samuel and the others

Not to worry, they said, it really wasn't a problem. Stana was a gifted and hard-working pupil, they said, and there was no risk, they stressed, no risk at all of her having to repeat the year.

Stana never stood in the corner, Stana never had to hold out her hands to be struck with a ruler. But because there was a set number of strokes and corners, all the corners and strokes that were Stana's due had to be given out elsewhere, and the upshot was that she could not choose her friends. When she thought about it, Florentine and the pastor were the only ones who weren't afraid of her father – and Samuel.

'They all confess,' Konstanty said once. 'Everyone has something to confess. Everyone wants to be guilty.' If they did not understand this at the start of the interrogation, then – and he made no secret of this – he had his ways to ensure that they felt a sense of guilt when they were finally released into prison or into what, even in these circumstances, was called freedom.

There was a logic beyond arguments. There was a logic of the night. A logic of desolation. A logic of blows. Blows aimed at the kidneys could be very effective.

'You leave the pastor alone,' Malva had said that summer, after the Jeremiah sermon. 'If you lock up the pastor, I'll leave. She's the only one I have left.'

Samuel's grandmother called Stana by her nickname.

'I'll leave out the 't',' Samuel had said one day.

From then on, she was Stana only to the others. To him, she was Sana. Because Sana meant dreamer and, in Arabic, 'the blue sky', which he liked even better. Samuel treated words as if they might wear out from overuse. New words were treasures, discoveries that belonged to him alone. Sometimes he would make a present of one, such as 'imponderables', for the things you couldn't calculate. He would point out an especially beautiful word: the Romanian 'greoaie,' cumbersome, an adjective that used five vowels to describe something very ordinary – and then there was 'oaia', sheep, which did without consonants altogether.

With this name, Stana became someone else. Sana was a gentle refraction; just a small change but what it referred to, what it encompassed was excitingly unknown. It touched something in her as yet unused, making her feel that she could reinvent herself. Something soft and generous was revealed, but also a new vulnerability, as if something was missing, as if it wasn't just that single upstanding letter he had kept for himself.

'Sana' said Samuel's grandmother in greeting, eyeing her with a regal severity all her own. She asked if she was eating enough, and for an instant Stana felt even more gangly than usual. Everything about Karlina seemed to be from another age. The hair pinned on top of her head, the handbag she carried in the crook of her arm. The way she lay down for a nap after lunch, stretched out on the divan with a handkerchief over her eyes. She had definite ideas. How to lie down, how to speak, how to eat, how to run a household. She beat the rugs in the pastor's house, releasing clouds of dust; she cut the heads off chickens and watched unmoved as they ran on, directionless, around the yard. Her soups with drops of oil floating in them were strained until they were clear as glass, a method no one else could master – something she never failed to mention.

With a sideways glance at her daughter-in-law, she said: 'Extraordinary that no one here can make a traditional soup.'

'What tradition do you mean?' said Florentine. 'Swabian, Slovakian, Hungarian, Romanian, Czech, Jewish, or Serbian?'

That Samuel and Stana were permitted to eat in the street (bread, cheese, tomatoes from the garden, sun-warm in the hand), signified a collapse of morals and manners in Karlina's view. Even when they'd had only one room, sharing kitchen and bathroom with other families, she had known how to organise things. Standards were to be upheld. But Karlina did not criticise, to avoid breaching the peace between her and Florentine, which had always needed negotiation, reinforcement.

Once after Karlina had beaten a rug and then gone home, Florentine had told Samuel and Stana to scatter sand over it. The pastor had not dared to contradict his wife or fetch the broom, and until the next snow fell, that sand had remained on the living room floor, a pale pattern working its way into the rug with every step.

On the evening of Karlina's arrival, they were invited to a party. The pastor's family, Stana's family, half the village.

A pig had been slaughtered. Though Stana couldn't bear the shrill, piercing cries of animals that guessed they were about to die, still an inexplicable euphoria overtook her. The people bustling about, the equipment standing ready: hook, saw, pail, wooden table, knife. A precise cut. The blood collecting. The flaying. The cracking of the breastbone. The sluicing of the yard.

Samuel disappeared after the meal. Stana sat between Ruth, who had come with her daughter and grandson, and Karlina, who chattered like no one else, a lavish back and forth of thoughts. Stana was used to Florentine and Samuel's companionable quietness, the heavy silence between her own parents. She enjoyed Karlina's stories and her incessant digressions, those foragings for understanding through which she sought to position herself and others. From the long white franzeller loaves that were handed round with the meal, she moved on to the royal palace, then to the region of Moldavia and, while she was there, to the poet Eminescu, to Queen Carmen Sylva, who had also written poetry (in the German language, admired by Theodor Roosevelt and Empress Elisabeth, as Karlina remarked with some pride), finally circling back to the garden, where a fire was now burning – and where Samuel was still absent.

Stana found him in the branches of the cherry tree.

'A million,' he said.

'Sorry?'

'A cherry tree has over a million petals.'

'What an extravagance,' she said, climbing up.

'It's exactly enough,' Samuel replied. 'Not one too many.'

Samuel had been making these comparisons ever since he had started labouring on a farm. He went to work almost every afternoon. Supposedly to learn about collective agriculture, but Stana knew it was because the farmer let him drive the tractor, and sometimes even took him up in his crop-dusting plane.

Stana sat beside him. That way she was close, without having to look at him. The understanding that had always existed between them was gone from his eyes. Something both precipitous and appealing had taken its place, something that resisted all efforts to name it.

Only now did Stana see what Samuel was holding. It was completely enclosed in his hand, with only a head showing. At first, she thought it was alive. Samuel passed the bird to her wordlessly. It was strangely light, almost incorporeal. She placed it carefully in the fork of a branch, and Samuel handed her a sprig of leaves to cover the lifeless body.

For a moment she closed her eyes, and knew that Samuel's eyes were closed, too. Things were almost like they used to be. She missed the usual gestures, those soft touches that had ceased almost entirely, without her quite realising when.

Stana looked pointedly out at the garden, although what was happening down below was of no importance. She focused her eyes on the guests standing by the fire, while bats arrowed through the garden, and was glad of the rustling leaves, which had once been cherries, which had once been a million blossoms, glad too that there was no need to speak. A laugh, the tinkle of glasses, a cry of, 'Your good health!', and someone launched into a song. Samuel slid closer. She slid closer. Or perhaps nobody moved, and it was the branches intertwining, their canopy of leaves fanning together, until they had to look at one another.

These strange moments had been happening for weeks.

Even in a cherry tree, you weren't safe.

Karlina rescued her.

'Come down you two, we're leaving,' she called.

"Come up,' said Samuel.

'If I climb a tree, I shall die,' said Karlina.

No one wanted to risk that.


Here and there, lights burned in the windows. Dogs barked behind gates. A bright moon deepened the shadows, turning roofs into strings of pointed bunting, electricity masts into ladders falling diagonally across the street.

'Whyever did you have to move to the end of the world, out here where the devil lost his hat,' Karlina grumbled.

Florentine and Malva were chatting; Hannes and Konstanty were not. Stana and Samuel did not speak, either. More than once their hands touched; they were walking very close together.

Stana began to walk up the electricity masts' shadow ladders, right across the street. She stretched her arms as if balancing at a great height, not looking down.

When they reached the gate of the pastor's house, Florentine invited them in for a nightcap. There was only one problem, and it could already be heard as they rounded the corner.

A polyphonic croaking from all sides.

Florentine could endure the mice in the larder, the moths in the bedroom. She made her peace with the ants in the hallway and shook the caterpillars from the washing. She swatted mosquitos and caught spiders. But she could not bear toads. Their oval black eyes, their warty brown skin. And worst of all, their long legs; she feared the way they sprang up at you, leaping out of nowhere.

Hannes crouched down. Florentine passed Karlina her handbag. Konstanty crouched as well and took Malva on his back, something he had never done before. Shaking her head, Karlina held Malva's bag as well, while the men piggy-backed their wives from the gate to the front door. Florentine flung out her legs exuberantly. Malva laughed, soft little pearls of laughter switching on a warm light in Stana's belly.

Toads chirruped from the grass and hedges, jumped across the path. A gleeful, carefree sound.

Samuel and Stana stayed behind until the adults disappeared into the hallway. Then Samuel pulled Stana to him.

# Macromolecular

. . . . .

It had not been his idea.

In the air.

In a propeller plane.

But it worked.

Oz had tried forged papers. It was reckless, it was stupid. But audacious, too. A friend had married a West German woman. On the day of the wedding, when the registrar left the room for a moment, Oz tore a marriage certificate from the pad of forms in plain sight, casually, as if he was sweeping breadcrumbs from the table. No one said anything. He rolled up the paper, put it in his shirt pocket. All evening he made sure no one hugged him too tight. Maybe he was sweating so much that no one wanted to. What he hadn't realised was that the sheets were numbered consecutively. Someone ratted on him. Anyone could have done it, including the bridegroom who was waiting for his exit visa.

A month after the wedding, he had travelled to the Black Sea. He had stopped thinking about that piece of paper, which was all it was, of course. It would only become something when he could put his name on it alongside that of a foreign woman (one he first had to find), when he had procured the official stamp, and then it became the possibility of leaving the country. Wiping away the border, the fixed routes.

How brave would a person be if they only dared?

The Persians named the points of the compass after colours. White the west, red the south, green the east, black the north. That was how the Black Sea got its name, Marea Neagră. Space was black, Luther's robe was black. But a black day was as undesirable as being on a black list. Which he was.

One afternoon on the promenade, a man came up to him. He was wearing a long-sleeved shirt. His shoes shone as if straight out of a dance lesson. Despite the heat, there wasn't a single bead of sweat on his forehead. He did not look like a holiday maker. Oz knew at once that this was not good.

'The registry office is closed.'

That was all he said.

Oz phoned Samuel. He told him where he had hidden the form, and instructed him to send it back to the registry office in an envelope. Nothing could be proven. And yet. Some veil had been lifted, something had turned its surprised face towards him. He took fright when someone asked for him, when footsteps rang out behind him. He heard those shoes tapping down corridors, or on the street at night. The doubling of his own tread. He kept seeing them in a crowded lift, on the tram, on the sidelines of a football field.

His flat was searched. He was brought in. The game was always the same. First, questioning by a bad-mannered policeman, who threatened a beating. Then a friendly policeman. I can help you: tell the truth. But the last thing these people wanted was the truth.

For a while, it was alright. Then Oz encountered someone who didn't threaten a beating, but gave one.

Just think about something else until it's over, he told himself. He offered up his face, not even raising his hands to protect it. The licking surf. The salt line on Erika's shoulders, where the ends of her hair fell. Stretched out curls. Eyelashes stuck together as after a long sleep. He bit into a lemon, pretended it was fine. When Erika laughed, he didn't care if she was laughing at or with him. The shudder sent through him by the lemon's acid. A delayed shudder that filled his whole body – like pain finally setting in and thickening everything.

His left eye was swollen shut. His chin smeared with blood. He locked the bathroom door, sat on the rim of the tub to take off his shoes. His fingers wouldn't move, his hips refused to bend. A knock at the door. With an effort, he got up and listened at it.

'It's me,' his sister whispered.

'Leave me alone, Thea,' he said, just as quietly.

He knew she was still there, because he didn't hear footsteps. And he, too, stayed where he was, ear held to the wood, leaning the way he used to years ago, when he would stand and stare at his mother's light pink dressing gown. It had hung on the bathroom door long after her death. Oz used to bury his face in it, the sleeves round his shoulders like a hug, until the dressing gown stopped smelling like her and then one day was gone.

Oz stared at the tiled wall. Counted the rows. If they came to an even number, he would... what? It was a childhood game his mother and Florentine had thought up, to shorten the wait to see officials. It didn't help.

Oz heard a silvery sound, and out of the corner of his eye caught a flicker of brightness. A musty, damp smell filled the bathroom.

Don't look, he told himself. Don't look. But then he did.

Outside the window, in the inner courtyard (earth wet from a shower of rain, gleaming roof shingles, wooden fences), scaly skin was moving. It slid past the window as if the house itself was on the move, and not the scales outside, until an eye appeared. Then everything stood still. Oz seemed to be falling – and when he came to, he was lying on the floor, the window once again framing a solid section of the world, courtyard, fences, roofs.

You're becoming one of those pathetic figures you used to pity, he thought. No one will do anything for you, because you can't do anything for them. And so it goes on for all time, no single person able to save another.

Oz had done his military service in a prison.

Being the best sharpshooter, he was stationed in the watch tower. The nights were better than the days. Apart from the odd light in a window, only fields lay before him, woods like a paper silhouette, and beyond only the church spire marked where the village was. The nights were cold, but not lonely like the days. The sky listened to him. A bird could be an answer. A woman walking across the fields in the morning. Mostly, nothing happened. Sometimes a prisoner was fetched for interrogation from the cells, cells with no pillows or blankets on their beds. Cells with buckets for toilets. He was surprised the men still needed to go, when all they had to eat was thin soup, semolina or corn porridge.

At the outermost point of this world, Oz kept watch.

Three square metres, gunports, a staircase.

One night as he was relieving himself through the port, a face appeared at a cell window. Someone who still had the strength to pull himself up on the bars, or the guts to stand on the bucket. Oz did up his flies, looked at the pale, moonlit face, the shorn head and dark, shining eyes like those of a child. The eyes were exploring their surroundings, the vastness of the night sky, the stars, the larches in the prison yard. It seemed to Oz that they were looking at him. He took a step back. The face vanished, but reappeared the following night. Oz grew used to this face; it became part of the night, and he wondered if he was part of this man's night as well, or if he was just imagining that the man could see him, was actually looking for him.

Did he hate him? See him as an ally? Oz was imprisoned too, in the watch tower, in the barrack rooms, in this country. He was ashamed to think these things, not wanting to compare himself with this man. And yet.

One night, the man didn't appear. The barred window stayed empty. The same the next night. And all the nights that followed.

They will have moved him, thought Oz, and did something he had never done: he inquired about the prisoner. He could work out the cell number, Block C, third floor, seventh window from the left.

'You want to be careful,' a soldier warned him. 'What's your interest in this man? Do you know him?'

Oz nodded. It wasn't even a lie.

The next morning, the soldier approached him in the washrooms. The prisoner had been found dead in his bed after an interrogation. He'd had a heart condition, if Oz got his meaning. Oz did.

He kept watch in his tower.

A vast sky.

An empty, barred window.

The smell had come first. Musty cold, like a forest lake. Then a silvery noise and a flickering that blinded like glare on a window pane. He lost his balance, fell, clung to ledges, then to the floor, as if it too could shake him off like a horsefly.

A reptilian eye filled the gunport. Its pupil a slit the colour of fire. Beyond the other port, hard green scales. These two glimpses formed a surmise, and then the tower itself dissolved, as if it, and not what lay outside, was the improbable thing. Oz saw the whole picture, the wings, claws, the forked tongue, he heard the scales scraping against wood. And all with such clarity that he knew, despite the fear and the dizziness, this was no dream.

In the morning, a woman walked across the fields.

Her boots left tracks in the earth. Her rucksack was empty and would presumably be full on the way back. Oz, who had righted himself, climbed down the stairs of the tower. He kept looking at the woman's tracks. There was another place here. A reason to cross the fields in the morning.

For the rest of his military service, Oz passed on secret messages and obtained cigarettes – the currency of every prison in the world. He mollified guards, sent signs of life to relatives. Nothing could help the man, bring him back, or bring Oz himself back to those nights when they had been the closest person to one another.

He moved back in with his father and sister; his brother Mirko now lived in Bucharest. Oz sensed the trembling of dragon's feet on the field, saw the shadow of a wingspan on the village roofs, heard the scaly skin, every movement bright and silvery. Sometimes the dragon didn't show itself for weeks. Then it reappeared, in the solitude of the plain or, worse, behind a person Oz was speaking to. He struggled mightily to pretend nothing was happening. But most people were practised in letting themselves be deceived.

Perhaps being deceived was the thing everyone most longed for.

As soon as his face looked normal again, Oz went to Temeswar to find 'the gardener'. While the Romanian state negotiated tariffs with West Germany for the emigration of Germans (even demanding compensation for education and travel costs), Securitate officers and Party comrades had also seen the opportunities for financial gain from all those waiting for their exit visas.

Oz was sent to the fortifications in the north of the city, where the Vienna Gate once stood. The streets were full of pigeons. They took over the boulevard, the opera house plaza, the cathedral square. A rippling grey mass, their jerking heads a reverse denial. A woman stood inside a flock, scattering food. Rain clouds hung ominously over the roofs. The colours slid into grey.

Oz leaned against a brick wall. Someone who had arrived quietly was suddenly leaning beside him, one leg casually bent.

'I'd like to speak to the gardener,' said Oz.

The man laughed. A brief, scornful laugh.

'I do understand,' said Oz. 'He has the aubergines to attend to. He doesn't have time for ordinary corncobs like me.'

Oz's sense of humour, which helped him even at times like this, irritated the man. But he quickly recovered.

'You pay 8000 deutschmarks to one of our men in Arad. Then we'll see what we can do for you. Do we have a deal?'

A slip of paper was pressed into his hand, with a name and a place written on it. Oz looked at the note, amazed at how little it weighed. Then he tore it into tiny shreds. He didn't know where he was supposed to get that much money. Anyway, you could be sent to jail for having western currency, and there was no guarantee it would speed up the paperwork. Despite the gardener's supposedly good contacts at the passport office, years could go by before an exit visa was granted.

Oz wondered whether the 'black man' in Hermannstadt or the 'warehouseman' in Agnetheln had different conditions. He could not show his face again with the gardener; the middleman made that obvious. And while he was considering what to do, weighing up options, making plans and then abandoning them, the house was searched. This time, they didn't even pretend they hadn't been there.

The shades on the standard lamps had been switched, the shoelaces of the shoes in the corridor were tied together. Oz's heartbeat seemed to come from outside himself, as if the very walls were pounding.

Thea helped clear up before their father came home.

'Make it stop,' she said.

Now it was too late for everything.

Too late to stay, as well.

Oz had concluded that absolutely everything was invented. Every system a product of imagination. The whole religion business, football, communism.

This country upheld an order that took effort to believe in (if you believed in it at all). And yet it was insisted upon as an objective reality. But there was no order that could not be replaced with another. The ten commandments might have been twelve, football goals square, the longed-for equality of all people a treasured inequality of a few. An existing order could be changed simply by inventing another.

And one man was better at inventing than anyone else.

The Son of the Sun loved his people. He loved them so much that he shielded them from the seven deadly sins. He shielded people from pride by preventing them from having their own opinions. Greed and avarice could not exist where everything was in short supply. Jars of jam and powdered milk on the shelves (spaced out nicely so they didn't look empty) were not tempting enough to stimulate avarice. Lust, lechery, rage and vengefulness were confined to a few high-ranking officials; they indulged in unchastity and hedonism while the blameless populace pursued humanity's golden dream. When propaganda was the staple diet, gluttony was unthinkable. Envy and resentment were excluded since nothing belonged to anyone, and everyone had the same as their neighbour. Only sloth escaped his control. Laziness, cowardice and ignorance – these sins were hard to keep in check.

The Genius of the Carpathians lived a modest life. The whole palace affair was really just happenstance. The place could easily have been smaller, but once you had a conference room, you had to have a ballroom. And when you were this popular, you needed countless guestrooms. When you had a wife but set some store by your independence, you needed two separate staircases. And when you loved your people, you also loved their art so you needed archives, exhibition rooms, a theatre. How fortunate that capitalists could now and then help you turn religious art objects into money.

The Conducător was interested in art. He was a man of feeling, sensitive, deep, merciful, tolerant. A man of words and deeds, a family man. So of course, when it came to distributing important offices of state, he kept things in the family. Because he clearly loved his people, he allowed them to idolise him on countless posters and pictures. The only thanks he expected was children. Women who sought an abortion were imprisoned, and if a forbidden termination gave them an infection, they were not to be treated. If you loved and wanted offspring, you had to be strict, and this pitilessness showed Oz how greatly the leader of this country in which he was forced to live devalued his subjects. He who lets others suffer must in his secret heart despise himself, but even this way of thinking about it could not explain why his mother had had to die.

A titan needed a titan queen. An ordinary girl from the poor suburban mahalas would not do. She had to be a scientist of global renown. Someone who was as skilled at acquiring doctorates as she was jewels. The state of the nation was discussed in the marital bed. There, they could add something (a new law), remove something (an old law). Best of all: whatever they did had a negligible effect! His Elena was an expert in macromolecular bonds. How practical, when in communism, as in macromolecular materials, everyone was naturally equal.

The Chosen One lived modestly. All his life, even as an apprentice shoemaker, he had refrained from earning money: was that not the proof of his frugality? The people were always moaning that there was nothing to buy. He himself had never bought anything in a shop. The Party looked after him. He and his Party comrades could earn a little on the side from selling off the Germans – who, to his amusement, went by the code name 'pădureni' (forest dwellers) in the Securitate correspondence. Though these sales ran counter to his own beliefs: Romania was not a country of emigration; if you were born here, you stayed. All nationalities were respected and had the same rights. And for those who still had itchy feet, his remedy was a world map displayed in Bucharest's National Museum, with coloured markers plotting his trips.

The Great Navigator was wise. He wanted his people to be proud of their role in history, conscious of their unique historical identity. And yet foreign countries were constantly trying to throw him off course. It was incomprehensible. If he wanted to drain a part of the Danube delta, Gorbachev complained. If some neighbourhood in Bucharest had to be flattened for his palace, it was immediately up for discussion at UNESCO. If word got out that he meant to dismantle a trifling seven thousand villages and relocate their inhabitants to new flats, built specially for the purpose to the standards of the time (systematisation being the watchword here), there was an outcry in the Western press.

Generally, mind, they let him do whatever he wanted.

The dictator's invented game needed many players. Soldiers, police officers, doctors, judges, prison guards, journalists – they would never, under any circumstances, admit that the order in which they lived was a product of imagination. And Oz knew that, until they did, there would be watch towers and prisons, shiny shoes and knotted shoelaces. There would be senseless laws, causing suffering that nothing could justify. There would be fear and, worse, the fear of fear.

He knocked and woke Samuel.

His friend asked no questions. A few minutes later, they were walking through the village's nighttime streets. The cold was like a too-tight embrace, every step taken against resistance. The tarmac was cracked, the earth soft, swallowing the echo of their footsteps. The houses looked dusty, colourless. The darkness was complete, a space that didn't seem to belong to the village.

They went to an abandoned farm. Sat in the barn on a discarded seed drill. Oz lit a cigarette, took a bottle from the inside pocket of his coat. If it burned your lips and calmed your thoughts, it was good schnapps.

Oz began to talk.

No one could listen like Samuel.

Then he said, 'The dragon is back.'

Samuel asked when and how. He asked how often it

appeared, and what its appearance did to Oz. Oz dared to tell his friend the truth.

When a strip of blue brightened the east, the birds woke, and everything that had unfolded at a distance – their meeting, their conversation – was joined back to the village, Samuel stood up.

'The dragon flies, doesn't it?'

Oz looked at him, uncomprehending.

'The dragon flies through the air,' Samuel repeated.

Oz nodded.

With that, it was settled.

Samuel got hold of the plane.

A propeller plane, used for dusting fields with pesticides. The farmer was in the know, had received a suitable gift and would report the plane stolen.

The difficult part was leaving without being able to say goodbye.

Oz left his father all his money. He left his mother's necklace under his sister's pillow, a moonstone pendant he had always claimed as his own, perhaps because he'd had the least time with Nika.

He left no messages, whereas Samuel wrote letters to his girlfriend and parents, efforts he was unhappy with even after several tries.

'A parting doesn't hurt less when everyone knows about it,' said Oz.

But Samuel insisted on these letters, and on his last visit to the pastor's house, Oz felt like a traitor. Samuel had been with Stana. He was pensive, absent, a little cold – and this was all the more striking because Samuel's unconditional attention was something Oz, like everyone else, took for granted.

The pastor got off his bicycle, cheeks flushed and a hat pulled low over his forehead, called out something across the yard that might have been a greeting, or a piece of news, and from the hallway Oz and Samuel watched Florentine come up from the garden to meet him, with her grace and her seriousness, neither guessing what would happen that night.

They flew between three and four, a time when even the border guards were tired. The sound of the propellers would give them away. But by the time the guards realised it was not a farmer dusting his crops at an unusual hour, they would be on the Hungarian side. They would fly low enough to stay under the radar. The fuel would take them as far as the Austrian border.

Samuel started the plane, and everything began to vibrate. The seat, the metal shell, the observation window, the harness. Samuel's hands around the centre stick vibrated; so did his arms and shoulders. Behind him Oz, who had often visualised this moment, realised that the scene had played out like a silent film in his head. He'd forgotten about noise. The plane rolled over the ground, gathering speed. The propeller roared, irregular, hiccupping. They took off with a mighty rattle, and Oz was sure that everyone could hear them, that this noise could be heard as far as the border, that people were coming out of their houses and even the cats, dogs and the sunflowers in the fields were craning their necks to look upwards. They would be discovered, shot down like a pheasant on a hunt.

The aircraft stood at an angle in the air. Oz's stomach lurched upwards. The horizon, the fields, the distance. The plane jolted, as if on a heavily pot-holed road. Samuel looked to the side, and they arced left. A tear rolled down his cheek. Pressure? The height? The parting? Fear? Oz knew what Samuel was giving up for him, what he was doing for him. Had always done – waiting for him after school, telling him it wasn't a bad thing to be alone, to be afraid (of other boys, teachers, PE lessons); the only bad thing was giving in to fear. Together they had climbed trees and made their first catapults, and he had learned to aim, feeling for the first time that he could defend himself. He shot and broke window panes, he shot and gave another boy a black eye. It got him into trouble, but it helped.

Samuel had given him his nickname. Oswald was too long, he said, and 'wald' meaning woods made no sense. But the magician Oz, whom he found in a book, took on many different shapes: a beautiful woman, a dangerous predator, a fireball. Everyone sees what they want to in you, said Samuel, that doesn't mean it's what you are.

Again and again, Oz had asked his friend if he was serious. If it was worth the risk. He didn't care what happened to himself, but if the plan went awry, Samuel's life would be ruined, and that could not be ignored. It would work, said Samuel, with a certainty Oz didn't have. It would work, and their families would follow after.

The flight was quieter now. Below them fields, the shadow of the propeller plane. A second, noiseless shadow. Then clouds covered the moon, and both shadows vanished. Samuel raised his hand: that was the sign. They were about to cross the border, the line that had determined their lives. It was so all-encompassing, their world had ended so absolutely at that place, that they would not have been surprised to see a line drawn through the landscape dividing one country from the other.

They had chosen an almost uninhabited area, some distance from guarded border crossings. Still, at any moment Oz expected machine-gun fire, that the plane would burst apart and fall out of the sky. If this didn't work, there was no alternative. He looked back. On the horizon, a presentiment of morning. A loud, ringing blue. Perhaps the thought came to him because everything was noise now. There was nothing but the roar of the propeller. The dawn grew louder. His hope grew louder. And when he realised how long they had flown undetected, and that below were Hungarian fields and Hungarian roads, he noticed that the dragon, which had been with them all this time, was struggling to keep up. It fell behind. Just a little way at first, then so far that Oz could barely see it.

With a hiss louder than anything else – the plane, his heart – the dragon departed. Oz laughed, a great, all-embracing laugh. A hysterical laugh. A hungry laugh. And Samuel laughed with him. He held the centre stick with one hand and raised the other in a fist. Oz clapped him on the shoulder. They laughed until their faces hurt, until Samuel got a stitch and Oz couldn't breathe.

No matter how often he checked the sky.

The dragon stayed away.

What followed could be counted on two hands.

Leaving the propeller plane.

Waiting for documents in Austria.

The story of their flight in the paper.

The onset of winter.

Travelling on to Germany.

Transit point for resettlers in Nuremberg.

Language test in the reception centre for refugees and resettlers in Rastatt. Result: fluent German speakers, language test not required.

Temporary hostel.

Spring.

The German they were hearing was rounded, with long vowels and a lot of sch sounds. It was unfamiliar, and they felt the foreignness of their angular, wayward pronunciation. They said Banat. And might as well have said Atlantis, Wonderland, Middle Earth. They said Romania. And were taken for Romanians, as if a country and the nationalities living there were one and the same.

They went out to buy food. Germans shopped in places large as warehouses. Their trolley stayed almost empty; the choice overwhelmed. They wanted to buy water and chose the wrong crate. The liquid was clear, with only a small tell-tale lemon on the label. Oz thought of all the times he had joined a queue at five in the morning and asked what there was today. With any luck, whatever it was would not just have run out when he reached the front. He was used to going from shop to shop, hoping for more than one ration. If you needed new shoes, the woman in the shoe shop would only sell if you had something to exchange.

Here, everything was available. Always. Once, when the Lyoner sausage had run out, the girl on the meat counter was so apologetic that Oz felt as if he should console her. Here, you waited at crossings for the green man, even when no cars were coming. Some people went running through the city, jogging on the spot at crossings until it was their turn to go. Oz joked that they were on the run from the Securitate. Some families had two cars while others had none, and rode bikes to save the environment. Oz theorised that because they had everything, both possession and renunciation demonstrated who you were, or wanted to be. And because there was so much of everything, two things had to be done at the same time: jogging and pushing a pram; watching TV and talking to guests. Here no one sat outside the house. No one dropped in unannounced, no one woke you without good reason, just to talk. There was too much of everything, and too little of something else: time.

You exchange something, leave something behind. You only know what that thing is once you've gone. And when Oz looked east, the horizon seemed to shimmer green.

'I want to go to the sea,' he said.

On a map of Germany, Samuel ran his finger along the coast. The East Friesian islands swung out like a string of pearls from the mainland. Oz tapped further up the map, pointing to an island that seemed large enough for a person not to feel lonely.

From the village, an avenue led to the sea. Past wheat fields, past trees whose evening shadows wandered across the ground. They were outsized. The low sun, the flat land stretched out their squat, knotted shapes turning them long-limbed. Oz had bought his bike at a flea market, repaired it and christened it Kobielsky. He thought this name both rakish and good-natured.

He liked the route back. To Samuel's mind, the way to a place (no matter where) was all anticipation; the return was marked by a vague emptiness. But Oz thought you should always go somewhere or other, just in order to have the way back. On the way back, those plans you had made were already behind you.

Everything that lay behind you was reassuring.

On the ride home, the wheat fields gold and green, the trees dancing their evening stilt dance, he felt the day inside his body. His fingertips alive from working in the public parks, muscles warm from pushing Kobielsky's pedals, skin tight from the hot sand, the cold of the sea – a surprising cold you were never quite ready for, even in summer. He liked the smell of the pine woods, the gentle upward slope of the sandy path through the dunes, feet sinking in, the sudden expanse of the beach. He liked plunging headfirst into the waves, without hesitating, so fast he was ahead of the cold. Then he forgot that his back hurt, that his colleague had called him a nancy boy when, using a noisy chainsaw, he'd asked for ear defenders. It sounded like an insult, though Oz didn't know exactly what it meant.

Before the way back came the way there.

And before the way there came the day.

And before the day came night.

Oz slept on a mattress on the floor, and so did Samuel. Their flat had a temporary feel. They could have packed in half an hour without leaving anything behind. Oz lay awake and thought about his family. People said the supply situation had got worse. That in the cities, electricity was turned off for hours at a time and everything was rationed, oil, potatoes, bread. He thought about the vast, fertile fields of the Banat and wondered why foreign countries were buying food from a place where people were going hungry. Defectors had difficulty staying in touch with their families. Samuel wanted his parents to apply for emigration, but Florentine refused. He wrote letters to Stana that went unanswered. Oz and Samuel spoke little about it. They had an agreement.

This was: we are here now. What matters is the Here.

The price was too high to allow doubt.

The sea now lay in all directions. But it was not black. When Oz closed his eyes and thought of a colour, it was a shimmering blue. Some nights there was a touch of green. Sometimes the face behind the bars appeared. Sometimes his mother's green eyes. Never the dragon. The propeller plane with the dragon alongside, two shadows moving over nocturnal fields near the Hungarian border – that was the last time he had seen it.

Once Oz had swum in the sea, as he did every day after work, he cycled to his favourite café. He parked the bike, ordered beer at the bar, and it was brought by a woman he hadn't seen before. Short curly hair, round glasses. She wore a dress with thin straps; one had slipped off her shoulder and it was exciting that she didn't seem to care. Oz couldn't utter a word. Stunned, he looked at her small white teeth, the fine lines around her eyes that showed how much she liked to laugh. He found a seat outside and lit a cigarette. At the next table, the island's bookseller was talking to another man. Under a chair, a dog dug itself into the gravel. Children were running between the tables. Oz saw and heard all this, yet he did not see and hear it.

He learned her name a week later. He and Samuel had run through a hundred scenarios for approaching her, but Samuel was not a good advisor in these things.

At some point she simply said, 'I'm Mina.'

'I'm Oswald. You can call me Oz.'

'Like the wizard?'

'Yes.'

'Where are you from?'

'The Banat.'

'Romania,' she said.

And he was glad he didn't have to explain.

All at once, the way back stopped being more important than the way there. The fields flew past, the trees grasped each other's shoulders, forming an alley. Kobielsky whirred. The disappointment when it wasn't her shift. The happiness when it was.

Even before he had said his prepared line, which in the moment of utterance collapsed into all its variants – would you like to, I don't suppose, how about, one evening, might you, I'd like to take – she said yes.

He wore his best shirt and trousers. Then felt embarrassed when he saw her. In a linen dress, a shawl draped carelessly around her shoulders, as beautiful as ever. He felt as if he was wearing his confirmation suit.

'You're serious about this,' she said, and laughed.

In the restaurant toilet, he took off his shirt. He was more comfortable in the t-shirt he was wearing under it. Later she took that off, too, with a gentleness and skill that unsettled him. Could you unlearn how to love a woman?

It was easier to learn to unlove yourself.

Samuel had not been easy to convince.

'I don't know her,' he said.

'That's the point. To get to know her.'

The evening was warm. The sea was calm. They strolled along the beach. Mina, her friend Freija, Samuel and Oz. In a sheltered spot, Mina spread out a blanket. Oz stuck torches into the sand, uncorked a bottle of red wine. He saw Freija move closer to Samuel and wished his friend was more talkative.

Say something, he willed silently, she thinks you're handsome. All women think you're handsome. Attracted by that combination of light, wavy hair and nut-brown eyes, silence, willpower and honesty. Oz was used to women always glancing at his friend, never at him. He saw their obvious friendliness at the supermarket checkout, the bank counter, in the café, their undisguised interest and the disappointment when Samuel withdrew, seemingly without noticing the efforts they made.

Freija asked Samuel questions, touched his arm as if by accident. Samuel tolerated her company, but there was no telling if he enjoyed it. He sat in the sand, legs bent, elbows propped on knees, turned half towards and half away.

Mina exclaimed and pointed at the sea, stretching out her arm.

The water was glowing. A green glow or was it blue? The breaking waves were washing a blazing liquid ashore. No, that didn't begin to catch it. Springing to his feet, Oz saw the whole shoreline glimmering, in snaking, constantly replenished ripples.

Mina wanted to swim. She didn't so much ask as declare it; this was an absolute. And while Oz was still lost in the spectacle, the others stripped off and ran into the sea. Too late to catch up. Undressing he felt clumsy in his underpants with his long, thin legs, and angry at having missed the moment, when of them all he was the fastest at plunging into the waves.

The water carried these thoughts away. The gliding blue-green was cold fire, like nothing he had ever seen. Every movement created it. From the beach they had seen only the line where sea and sand met, but now the water glowed around him, around his belly, his arms and hands. Freija leaped and fell back, a foaming spray of light. Samuel scooped up water with his hands. Mina swam to Oz, trailing a flood of light. They splashed each other wildly, then she pressed against him. She shook her hair; sparks dusted the water. It excited him, took strength not to give in to the impulse, the urge. They kissed, the water darkened again, and for one blink of an eye he thought he'd seen something in the waves.

Their footprints glowed on the beach. Freija dried herself with a towel. Samuel crouched on the shoreline. A name appeared in the sand, until a wave obliterated it.

Sana. In capitals.

Lust hit Oz full force. Mina had a way of seducing him, making him wait until the excitement became unbearable. Her self-confidence impressed him. She walked naked around the room, unashamed, sat on the toilet while he brushed his teeth. She carried heavy beer steins in the café, took the money, always ready with a remark. Sat down in the middle of the pavement to smoke a cigarette, careless, defiant. When she lay on the bed, eyeshadow smudged, not sucking in the dome of her belly, and he caressed her breasts, her firm, white skin, he knew he would never get enough of her.

The three of them went hiking. They stayed in a tent, Mina in the middle, he and Samuel on the edges. The tent was open, night air flowed in, a beetle straying with it. Oz lay awake listening to the irregular buzz. A warm hand rested on his thigh. The skin grew hot, heat radiating through his body, and just when he could no longer stand it, the hand began to move. Feeling around, seemingly without intent, then regularly. He tried to control his breathing; a muted sound escaped him. He didn't care that Samuel was sleeping next to them, he wanted to kiss her, wanted to roll onto her and make love noiselessly, but she pushed him away.

'It's too soon,' Samuel said a few weeks later. That sounded like: she doesn't love you. Oz had told him that he wanted to move in with Mina.

His friend's words stung. An argument followed in which he accused Samuel of not letting people in, being jealous of his girlfriend, of preventing him from making a life of his own. He accused him of using the escape as an experiment, just to find out if he could make it across the border. And now they were here, he wanted to go back, to betray everything they had risked their lives for.

That Samuel didn't defend himself made Oz angrier still.

He convinced himself that he was in the right, though he knew exactly what Samuel had left behind for his sake. He didn't want to be reminded. He'd had his fill of guilt.

'You've never accepted Mina.'

'She is not as serious about this as you hope,' said Samuel.

'How do you know that?'

Samuel tried to dodge the question, but Oz kept pressing him until Samuel confessed that on that tent night, Mina's hand had touched him, too. That he had felt her caressing both him and Oz, and had eventually pushed her hand away – he'd wanted to do it earlier, but been unable to.

'Eventually, how convenient,' said Oz.

He remembered Samuel sitting by the fire in the morning with his book, as he and Mina crawled out of the tent. His face was pale, and he hadn't said a word until lunchtime. This silence made him beautiful. This silence made him distant. The knowledge that his friend had enjoyed Mina's hand that night excited him in a way he could not pin down, a melding of lust and anger, although it was something he could never forgive him for.

That night, Samuel's bed stayed empty.

'Where were you?' Oz asked.

'Looking at the water, imagining how all the seas and rivers and streams flow together.'

That was a typical Samuel sentence.

They pretended the argument had never happened. But it had, and it left a crack that, despite all efforts, kept them from being close.

Throwing Samuel's advice to the winds, Oz asked Mina.

They were lying in bed, smoking. He wasn't certain she had heard him. He repeated the question.

'Do you want to move in together?'

He didn't want to keep arranging meetings, wondering when he would see her again. He wanted to see her every morning. Getting ready in the bathroom, putting on her clothes, making phone calls, sitting with her knees pulled up in front of the television. Waiting impatiently for him at the door because he'd dithered over what to wear. He wanted to stay up until she got home from the late shift, to cook for her, care for her, to always be there.

Mina smoked without looking at him. She stubbed out the cigarette, gave no answer. When they made love the second time he came too quickly. In her sleep, she turned away from him.

On the evenings that followed, she worked at the café. On the third evening she was tired. On the fourth evening he rode over to her flat, and at the door her flatmate said she wasn't in. He smoked under the streetlight, looked up at her window and thought he saw the curtains move.

The gestures of rejection.

Eyes too swiftly turned away. A voice that slipped into sympathy. The friendly touch on his forearm. Fleeting little kisses on the cheek.

He rebelled against this withdrawal. He explained, apologised, wooed. One evening, waiting outside the café at closing time, leaning on Kobielsky, he saw her come out onto the street with a strange man. His arm was around her, and while Oz was wondering what that meant, they kissed.

Oz got drunk in a bar. Fell into conversation with two men, went with them to another place, but when he came back to the table with a round of beers, they were gone. A man at the next table gave him a searching look and crossed his legs. His shoes shone, the toes pointing towards him as if to say: there you are.

Oz was in pain, without being able to say where it came from, and he remembered how he had put his hands on his mother's belly to stop it hurting. He saw a cell window in the moonlight, a face that appeared on the other side, until one day it no longer appeared and was no longer there.

Kobielsky's light flickered. The bike buzzed as it went over uneven places, loose cobbles, roots under the tarmac. Oz pushed the pedals, his calves burning. On the fields, the dance of the stilt trees. On the sea, a faint trail of silver, from the shore to the horizon. Oz dropped his bike in the sand.

The water was dark. Connected to everything.

Marea Neagră.

Oz swam a long way out.

He always had the feeling that a counterweight existed somewhere, standing in his way, throwing him off course, pushing him to the edge. Why should he set his own strength against it?

A whirling motion in the waves. The smell of a cold forest lake. Silvery bright scales, fire.

Lie on my back, the dragon whispered. I'll take you with me.

'Is it far?'

The dragon knew about distance.

# Jupiter

. . . . .

Bene's aunt ran a bookshop. In a thatched building not far from the station, in one of the island's prettiest villages.

At first he unpacked books, labelled, sorted, dusted, helped with the accounts. When his aunt had an accident – a careless step from a stepladder – and spent several weeks in hospital, he ran the place on his own. It seemed he had a talent for it. When, even after a rest cure, his aunt could no longer work full time, Bene took over the shop.

He did away with the alphabetical order, laid books out on tables where they could be clearly seen, added schnapps and fripperies to the stock, bought postcard stands. He put sheepskins down in the children's department; a rocking horse and a wing-backed armchair moved in. His aunt thought it excessive – a bookshop was neither a creche nor a souvenir stand – but since the customers were predominantly women who were clearly sweet on her nephew, she left him to it.

Success proved Bene right.

If someone wanted a book to cheer them up, he knew the very thing. If someone said they weren't too fond of reading, he might wonder what they were doing in a bookshop, but still took up the challenge. If a man came in asking for 'The Name of the Tulip', he cleared up the botanical confusion without lecturing. If a woman asked for 'A Hundred Years of Servitude' or 'Sons and Brothers', he was able to interpret and spent longer than usual chatting.

His own recommendations were laid out on a round table. Classics, contemporary literature and, of special significance to Bene, East German literature. Johnson and Fries and Wolf, at any rate. Also literature from Eastern Europe: Pastior, Bánffy, Marai, Kafka. What were bookshops good for if not personal recommendations? The temptation to talk everyone into buying a book from the round table was great, but it was smarter to ask the right questions and find out a customer's preferences and interests. Once you knew, there was nothing to stop you pushing the boundaries a little. It didn't always work. Bene led some customers straight to the overrated books category, those works passed from hand to hand that were supposedly impossible to put down, the voice of a generation – and not at all enjoyable, though the purchase of them was a mark of distinction.

Then again, the important thing was that people bought books.

Lending books was an abomination. People should own them. Reading a borrowed book was like having sex with your clothes on. It could be done, of course, and was even fun sometimes, but there was no comparison with being able to kiss and touch every last inch of skin. Only in your own books could you underline, dog-ear the pages, note thoughts in the margin, insert slips of paper, leave rings from coffee mugs or wine glasses. There was a reason for calling pages a body of text.

Bene found it hard to keep his cool when two customers were chatting about their current reading and one said to the other – quietly, so he wouldn't hear, but never quietly enough – that he could lend him the book. Lend! You could lend a car, money, an electric drill or a lawnmower. But books? Books could only be borrowed with the firm intention of never returning them, no matter what.

If their former owner should ask after them, you could pretend to be deaf, innocent, forgetful, moronic – whatever you chose, it had to be a dismissal.

That book? I gave it back ages ago.

Your book? Never had it.

A book was not the same after you had read it. If Bene lost a book or lent it to someone who had presumably taken his particular views on board, he was forced to rebuy and reread it, to make it *his* again. God preserve him from a house fire and with it, the necessity of rereading all his books. He had left his library behind once before.

And to his mind, once was enough.

Bene had a memory for books.

No, books *were* his memory.

They preserved the time in which he'd read them.

On one holiday, the last they took as a family, thin walls had revealed the state of his parents' marriage. Bene befriended Erich Kästner, learning that both bravery and its lack were to be exercised as discreetly as possible. At the end of that summer, his father moved out. Bene helped his mother, clearing out cupboards, rearranging furniture, taking the rubbish out. Both went to their own rooms to weep. To offer comfort was like making a racket in the morning – it wasn't good to start too early.

The smell of chlorine and the feeling of bare feet on wet tiles. Instructions yelled through the indoor pool, water spraying. The imprint of swimming goggles, still visible on the bus. Warmth, weariness, burning shame. The boys laughing in the showers, back-slapping, calling each other by their surnames. Küri, they called him, short for Küring. He liked it. The way they soaped themselves, teased each other, shook the water from their hair, and he joined in, pretending his looking was unintentional. A stray glance, taking in something that had always been there, but had changed over time, shoulder bones, upper arms, hips, and that place that marked the end of torso and belly and the start of something that elicited a clear, undeniable longing.

There were no coincidences, Bene read in Hesse's *Demian*; a person was only afraid when he wasn't at one with himself. Bene gave up swimming once he had his level three badge. Even now, when the blue paperback edition passed through his hands, he had that sense of sitting on the bus in the early dark of an autumn afternoon, limbs tired, hair wet, with the exciting, frightening realisation that he was different.

The sofa of his first shared flat was stained, the cushions threadbare, the cover unaired. He could not associate Dulcinea with roses; for all time, her aroma would be dust and mothballs. World literature needed to be associated with different seating. His flatmate Inge's rocking chair, for instance, a park bench, or the library, where books had to be disguised with socialist covers. Was Schiller comfortable wrapped in Marx's red robe? Bene decided to forgive the Swabian poet for rhyming freshwater fish into his oceans, since he'd only travelled there in his imagination. Schiller was a comfort to him. If as a schoolboy this writer had been called an average intellect, then Bene, too, could become someone.

Bene tried to become someone. First, though, he became fat. It might have been a lack of exercise, poor diet (cheap cabbage, bacon and eggs), and also because though reading might get you about a lot, it unfortunately didn't burn many calories. In Benjamin he had read that some places did not join seamlessly to the household – one such being the bed after a long period of illness. He feared that his passion for books was similarly poorly connected to what people called life. He went to university, did his share of the housework, cycled around the city, and could not shake the feeling that at any given moment, the adventure was always happening where he wasn't. If he stayed at home, he missed a legendary party. If he went to a party, it was one that no one even talked about the next day. Whatever he did, wherever he went, life had gone elsewhere. But with books, he was in the middle of things. The action only happened when he was there, and when he wasn't there, it waited for him.

He met Lothar in the queue outside the Colosseum.

Lothar, who went to the cinema as often as Bene, who wondered one day whether his flat was water damaged, uninhabitable. The two of them were turned away because the screening was sold out.

Bene could not get over Lothar's voice.

It was a voice that was perfect for lines such as, 'Frankly, my dear, I don't give a damn.' Or, 'If I want the birds to drop dead from the trees, the birds will drop dead from the trees.'

Bene fell into bed at night with a pounding heart. That came from all the coffee he drank, and also because it was impossible to be in love *and* eat regular meals. He was losing weight. His former body was revealed again, which was a good thing, and because he liked it, Bene returned to swimming. To shower he chose a single cubicle.

Lothar wasn't interested in long conversations. He took a firm position, was quick to reach a verdict when decisions had to be made. His tenderness was strong and certain, beyond all hesitation or restraint. He taught Bene what lovers do when they are not a man and a woman. Life happened wherever they were: in the cinema, the theatre; they went on trips where life condensed, suspending time and removing all aims. If Bene was overcome by doubt or uncertainty, one look into Lothar's eyes would lift him up again.

He didn't know they were subject to the same dangers as other couples. What happened to others could happen to them.

While Bene graduated and taught middle-school German and geography, Lothar dropped out of university, became a communications engineer and joined the Socialist Unity Party. He lost interest in going to the cinema, travelling, and in being seen in public with Bene. One evening he said he wanted them to separate. Bene saw in Lothar's face, where his nose suddenly loomed strangely large, that the separation did not lie in the future, and it wasn't happening now; it had long since happened. That morning when he left the house they must already have separated, and he wondered why he hadn't noticed the separation, why he had to be informed of it, though it had split their life, and him, in two.

The flat became his refuge. He tried to read, but neither Seghers nor Canetti could reach him. He looked out of the window, saw mothers walking their children home, groceries being delivered, boys sitting on the kerb and birds in the trees, just as they always had, as they always would, no matter what became of him. He ate pasta or rice just to avoid hunger, drank his way through the reserves of wine and spirits. The flat detached itself from the building, the street and the city, becoming a cut-off place where a man in a dressing gown looked out of the window and did not know how to rejoin his life to groceries, mothers, boys, birds.

There were different kinds of loneliness.

The loneliness of the mountain that had always been there. Of the wide-open plain where you felt lost. Of the city and its indifference. There was the loneliness of the staffroom, the overcrowded tram, the empty flat. The loneliness brought on by accusations, accompanied by words like 'never' or 'always', no matter whether they came from other lips or your own. The loneliness after his father left and when, years later, his mother died and he realised he had no one left. But the greatest loneliness of all was abandonment. The emptiness where another person had been. Everything had to be reinvented: how to get through the day, what to eat, who you were.

You had no idea what a state of grace you lived in when you weren't being abandoned.

Bene packed a rucksack (the only book he put in was the Rome travel guide), took a late train to Potsdam and hitchhiked from there to a service station on the East-West transit motorway. There he climbed into an unlocked lorry, hid in a box of toys – and in this way he reached the West. Border guards searched the lorry, and would have found him, had their sniffer dog not vomited on some of the goods they'd unpacked, which led to an argument and a premature halt to the search. Only then did Bene realise what danger he had put himself and the lorry driver in. His escape had been a series of rapid decisions. Decisions were no longer the preserve of Lothar.

In later life, you might not care to revisit the books of your youth – but a person who wasn't at one with himself was still afraid.

This man is just looking, was his first thought. Comes into the shop, browses, fingers the covers, reads a little (waiting to be accidentally seduced by a few sentences), looks at blurbs and author photos. Finally glances at the counter and leaves with a polite goodbye. He had never bought anything, or said anything. But he was beautiful.

At least the man was nice to watch, thought Bene.

There were plenty of things he'd like to watch him doing.

A browser might pinch something if you took your eye off him – which Bene, however, only pretended to do. He knew how to look busy while keeping something or someone under observation, a skill that had always been useful. He called this gameshow-host vigilance his Fritz Egner Face. It was good to put on different faces, smarter than relying on the one you were born with, since that one brought the worst luck. Though of course, he didn't like to admit it. Especially not to men.

This guy must work on the docks. He was wearing rubber boots and a raincoat. He also smelled of fish. The scent of fish among the books was not especially welcome. But Bene couldn't send him away, either; he was a potential customer. And he was too good-looking. A less attractive man smelling of fish would not have been allowed to browse as long.

Maybe I'll put out a box for books that don't sell, Bene thought. One mark each.

And, a few days later, the guy actually slid E.T.A. Hoffmann's *The Golden Pot* across the counter, along with a coin.

Every autumn Bene threw a party in the bookshop and, without thinking, he issued an invitation.

'Why?'

Bene was so surprised at this reaction that he began to stutter. The guy had just bought his first book. And it was from the one-mark crate. What a crazy, entirely obvious come-on.

'Thank you.'

It didn't sound like a yes.

Despite the cold, Bene opened a window. He thought about his time in West Berlin, before (having spent enough time in a city with a wall) moving to live with his aunt by the sea. Bene had lodged with a man who travelled a lot on business. When he was away, Bene left the flat exactly as it was. Didn't even retune the radio, although classical music did nothing for him. It was a relief to live like someone else. Someone who had a favourite radio station, cacti, a colour scheme, someone who had arranged his life in this way and no other. Bene kept his head above water working in a rubbish separating facility. The smell clung even after he left for the day. This isn't just a job, it's what you *are*, he thought. But it wasn't bad work. You passed the time telling jokes, secretly passing a hipflask around, opening up porn magazines as a greeting to the people further down the conveyor belt. No one could know that bare breasts had no effect on Bene.

Bene stood at the window, watching the dock worker cycle away, and thought: there's another person smelling of a life he never dreamed of having.

The wall fell.

The whole eastern bloc, Hungary, Poland, Bulgaria, Yugoslavia, the Czechoslovak Socialist Republic, was on the point of disintegration, because the Soviet Union had chosen reform. Only in Romania did a leaden calm reign.

The Iron Curtain was shattered, so it was said, and Bene thought about how naturally people lived in metaphors. Even something that had ruled the lives of countless people for decades could fall, could shatter, and he wondered whether metaphors hid experiences or made them evident. If you spoke about a thing differently, would you experience it differently?

People asked Bene why he wasn't going to Berlin. He said he couldn't shut the shop. His aunt offered to fill in. No need for that, said Bene; it was impossible now, anyway, just before the Christmas rush.

Every evening, he taped the news and all the special broadcasts on his video recorder. Images of people tearing down fences, being pulled up onto the wall, embracing, idle border guards, the bluish sheen of Frau Honecker's hair.

It was a mild autumn, with no snow. A fizz of purple spread over the heath. Here and there, a rosehip still clung to the bushes. The houses hunched in the wind, their thatched roofs like woollen hats pulled low over forehead and ears. The dune grass was a November yellow. Beyond it, nothing but sea, sky and sand. The rush of waves, the sound of your own footsteps. Perhaps a seagull. Bene strode out like a man with somewhere to be. His pace slowed only gradually. So did his thoughts. And then he let in the sadness that always came when it was so quiet, so empty, so lonely, so complete, so beautiful.

Parts of Berlin that for years he had visited only in memory were suddenly within reach again. Mitte, Friedrichshain, Prenzlauer Berg. He had not so much left a place, he now realised, as a design for life. The middle-school teacher who tries his luck at the Colosseum of an evening, who cycles along the Panke, reads books hidden in plain covers. The swimming club man who dives, crawls, swims on his back, jumps from the rim into the water a zillion times and climbs back out. Always among the last in time trials. That was the life envisaged for him. Inventing a new one had taken strength and, now that the borders were open, he no longer knew what he was intended for.

Bene concentrated on walking, bending from time to time for a shell. There were not many footprints. Most were cut into the sand with an energetic heel; others even, as if made by someone holding back his full weight.

At first, he was just an outline. Then Bene saw that it was a man in a yellow windcheater. Crouching, his face in his hands.

Bene stopped.

The man raised his head.

It was the one-mark guy.

'Is everything alright?' Bene asked, the way you do when things are all wrong.

'I'm thinking about a friend.'

Something in the sound of his voice – his German sinking softly into the words – moved Bene to crouch down beside him. He watched him from the corner of his eye. A clear profile that could be drawn onto paper with a single line. Straight eyebrows, small ears. Reddened nose and eyes. The salt, the cold.

They looked at the water. A cutter carried a bow wave in front of it.

When it began to rain, they walked across the dunes back to the road.

'I'm Bene.'

'Samuel.'

They shook hands formally.

When Bene picked Samuel up from work, he treated himself to fresh oysters. He liked the shells, like something from the dawn of time, the wet, salty taste. That taste was too intimate for Samuel. He washed mussels in a tin tub (a sandy, rattling sound), sorted the catch of the day, picking the fish out and laying them carefully on crushed ice.

He had never been out to sea.

They went to the cinema, the only one on the island. The new James Bond had been showing since the summer. You could always watch Timothy Dalton. Bene's films of the year were *Steel Magnolias* (Sally Field and Julia Roberts in one film!)

and *The Big Blue*. If you saw that film on the island and didn't fall for the dreamlike images of the sea or fall hopelessly in love, there had to be something wrong with you.

It soon became clear that Samuel was not into men. Bene hadn't had a steady relationship since Lothar; a few dalliances, mostly holidaymakers. Options were limited among locals. He didn't believe in platonic relationships between men, and secretly hoped that persistence would bring about the desired state, or maybe just time, as with Harry and Sally.

Once, while they were out walking, the zip on his jacket snagged. He pulled at it until the zip was completely ensnarled and wouldn't go up or down. The wilfulness of things could make him unreasonably angry, and he was seconds away from pulling the jacket over his head and throwing it to the ground. Then Samuel came over. He stood so close that Bene caught the scent of his hair – floating, gentle, no hint of fish – and worked on the zip with a patience that both impressed and unsettled.

How long had this calm dwelled within Samuel? Had he brought the same serenity to averting arguments, concealing fears, to his first kiss? What if he took Samuel's head in both hands now, lifted his chin, looked into his sand-coloured eyes until he relented? Their lips would open; he would be able to taste something of the coolness in Samuel's mouth, touch something that was hidden.

Samuel stood before him, head lowered, carefully teasing the zip until it released.

'Thank you,' Bene murmured, and walked on ahead. What are you doing, he thought. The guy is fifteen years younger than you. He doesn't want anything from you. And anyway, he never says a word.

Bene liked the way thoughts arranged themselves when you spoke. He felt alive in conversation. He never even tired of talking to customers, day in, day out, conversations that often led away from books to what people were experiencing, what occupied them. A good bookseller knew things about his customers.

Samuel's utterances followed long silences. And when he spoke, there was nothing to grasp hold of or correct. His silence was not deliberate, but to Bene could sometimes feel like a punishment. In other people, taciturnity bored him. But in Samuel, it was beautiful. It arose from long loneliness, and only someone who had himself been alone could recognise it for what it was.

Bene stayed behind in the bookshop, went walking on his own, picked Samuel up from work less often, as if to convince himself that he did not need this man's presence. Samuel understood the signs. When he stayed away from the shop for a while, Bene abruptly felt foolish. He booked cinema tickets (he always booked, although experience told him that they never sold out) and picked Samuel up from the mussel basin.

'Isn't your job boring?' he asked him one day.

'Nothing is boring,' Samuel said, and meant it.

What Samuel did, he did with concentration, as if nothing was more important, from making sandwiches to tying shoelaces. Sometimes this childlike earnestness made Bene laugh, but he valued the patience that came with it. Bene refused to wash up straight after dinner, but insisted that the blanket be folded after leaving the sofa. A rumpled sofa blanket bothered him. Samuel never commented on his book-filled bathtub (reminiscent of André Gide) or on his obsession with Rome which, Bene suspected, stemmed from his mother having given him a Catholic name. As he saw at the fish market, Samuel could rub along with everyone – the grouches, gossips, braggarts and brown-nosers – of both sexes. Only lateness made him fly off the handle.

When Bene kept turning up over fifteen minutes late, he was greeted with:

'Time is a thing you should never steal from someone. You can't get it back. Not the time spent waiting for someone, not the time of empty promises, of stalling.'

Though Bene promised to do better, he didn't know how. You only arrived late when something unforeseen happened. How were you supposed to foresee the unforeseeable?

One afternoon, they were in Bene's Ford Fiesta on the mainland. Recently the spark plugs had been playing up, and Bene noticed the engine stuttering, about to flood again. Samuel turned up the radio. The Free Europe station had news from Romania. There was a report on unrest in Temeswar. Demonstrations were spreading, thousands had taken to the streets in Arad, and now in Bucharest. The army was training water cannon on them and shooting live rounds, but there were also reports of solidarity with the revolutionaries.

For the first time, Samuel spoke about his parents, and Bene saw a garden before him, a kitchen where card games were played, a well, a flight of steps, a woman. He asked the name of the village and recognised the pastor's house where he had stayed with Lothar in the early seventies.

Bene took his foot abruptly off the accelerator.

Car horns blared behind them.

Realising they had met before, Bene as a student, Samuel as a little boy, they started laughing. Bene had never heard this laugh from Samuel. It came from his belly and shook his whole body. When they had calmed down, Samuel gave him a look that contained gratitude, friendship, a trace of relief.

A song was playing on the radio, one of those from the pop charts. Take a good look at yourself, it said, could you really sell out a new lover? The engine stuttered, the car slowed, Bene coasted towards a parking space. Samuel closed his eyes, leaned his head back. His clear, wilful profile stood out once more, so sharply that it pained Bene.

Samuel didn't seem to notice that the engine was no longer running and they had come to a stop.

Only when Bene laid a hand on his shoulder did he open his eyes, like someone who didn't know where he was.

'Šesťsto,' said Samuel, adding up the figures in his head.

Bene slid the sheet of paper underneath the others and put on his Fritz-Egner face – busy, innocent. Finally, unable to withstand Samuel's gaze, he admitted it was a customer's bill.

'It looks like he's never paid for a book.'

'Nor has he.'

Samuel had come to the bookshop after closing. He browsed the tables, read a few lines, put the books back – perhaps a little more desultory, a little hastier than usual – and finally walked over to the counter, where Bene was busy tidying up. It had been a good day, plenty of customers not needing to be convinced that books made an adequate Christmas present.

Bene didn't know why he kept the list. He would never ask the customer for this sum, which had now reached a high three figures.

'He's a poet,' he said, as if that explained it.

'And that's why he's allowed to run a tab?'

'Konrad can run a tab because I know that every book he wants is sensational. If he orders a book, I get twenty copies delivered right away. That's our deal. And I have no idea whether he knows that, or just thinks I'm a mug.'

It was only through Konrad that he had discovered Infante's *Three Trapped Tigers*, that melancholy, exuberant, chaotic, audacious beacon of literature. Konrad had been the first to ask for *Perfume*, well before it settled into the bestseller lists for years.

'I think every bookshop should have a Konrad,' said Bene, putting an end to the discussion.

'And sea buckthorn schnapps,' Samuel added.

Bene invited him to stay for supper.

He only realised that something was wrong when they were upstairs. Samuel cut the bread at an angle, and when the jar of gherkins refused to open, he just put it back in the cupboard. They ate in front of the television. When the evening news brought reports from Romania, Bene pressed the record button.

Candles burned on the table, strings of lights shone in the windows, and Bene and Samuel watched young demonstrators shouting, 'Down with Ceauşescu'. Then came footage of soldiers in the occupied palace, the socialist insignia removed from their caps and uniforms. The newsreader announced that the dictator and his wife had fled.

Samuel asked if he could use the phone.

Breaking one of his own rules, Bene went into the kitchen and washed up. When he had finished, he listened at the door. Silence. Samuel was sitting motionless on the sofa, the phone in his lap. Bene went to the bookcase, quietly, so as not to break the silence, pulled out a book and sat down beside him. The cover depicted Jupiter, Rome's protector, abducting Europa in the shape of a bull, seducing Leda as a swan, carrying off Ganymede as an eagle. Of its own accord, the book fell open at the page with the vine leaf, between the Trevi Fountain and Piazza Navona.

'I spoke to my mother,' said Samuel.

'What did she say?'

'Come home.'

His aunt helped out on the morning of 24 December. Then the shop was closed for a week. Bene stuck a notice to the door: We are taking a Christmas break.

The rain poured down. On the outskirts of Hamburg, they made slow progress. The windscreen wipers were loud, and Bene switched lanes impatiently. As they approached Hannover, he had a sudden urge to drive to Berlin, ring the bell at his old flat, walk through the rooms. He'd often wondered what had become of his books and furniture.

Samuel's coat was much too thin and, unlike Bene, he had brought only a small holdall. Bene had filled the rear footwell, which always had books in it, with new stock. He might need a book himself to dispel the silence, the doubt, the time. Or someone might ask for one; now the border was open, stories might need travel, not just people and goods.

The noises inside the car were loud, conversation almost impossible. They shared the driving. Bene was always loath to give up the wheel, but Samuel drove his Fiesta as if he'd never done anything else. He drove with foresight, anticipating others' mistakes, keeping his distance. He drove fast.

On the other side of Dresden, the weather improved, and Samuel grew more talkative. Near Brno, they found themselves in a conversation lighter and more effortless than any previous one. In Bratislava they picked up a hitchhiker, a Slovakian woman, and Bene was surprised to find that Samuel spoke fluent Slovakian. His voice was different in that language, firmer, more rapid. There seemed to be more words in Slovakian. The conversation went on and on, and Bene, who at first had tried to work out the odd word, settled back and let the unfamiliar sound wash over him.

They decided to spend the night at a motel in Szeged, and cross the border the next day.

The only room left was a double. Bene concealed his self-consciousness by talking without pause. He sang loudly as he showered, and out of tune, perhaps because the wall bar and the showerhead were mismatched and he had to bend down to wash his hair. When he came out of the bathroom with a towel around his waist, Samuel's eyes rested on him longer than he could find a reason for. Bene went to his bag, removed the towel and got dressed. When he turned around, Samuel was busy looking out of the window.

A plastic Christmas tree stood in the dimly lit dining room. Bene's mixed salad consisted of a chopped cucumber and a chopped pepper. Samuel ordered orange juice with his goulash soup and was given Fanta.

The evening news informed them that Ceauşescu and his wife had been sentenced and executed. They ordered schnapps and drank it leaning on the bar, each sunk in his own thoughts.

They waited for six hours at the border near Nădlac. They could see transporters filled with aid, bearing Hungarian, German and Austrian numberplates. The Fiesta was beckoned out. The border guards searched the car, asked if they had any ţigări. Cigarettes. Their papers were checked. One of the soldiers took Samuel aside. Bene saw Samuel remove his watch and hand it over.

Then they could carry on.

'What was that about?' Bene asked.

Samuel thought the soldier must have seen in his passport that he was a defector.

'How brazen, to ask for your watch.'

'He just asked the time, cât aveţi oră?'

'That's not brazen, that's elegant,' said Bene.

A few kilometres on they passed a military checkpoint and were searched again. The traffic only thinned out when they left the main roads. Here, too, there had been no snow, just rain. On a badly tarmacked country road, the sun appeared. Beams of light touched the fields, brought out their colours, limp green, violet-brown, copper. In this sudden light, the landscape seemed unreal. Bene felt his tiredness, felt the night in which he'd lain awake, as Samuel had, both pretending they were asleep. Something about this landscape moved him, the vastness, the unprotected open space, as if it was just a transition.

'Pull over,' said Samuel.

He threw open the passenger door even before the car had stopped. Bene's first thought was that his friend felt sick. The passenger door slammed shut. He knocked at the window, asked if everything was alright. When no answer came, he reached for the coats on the back seat. There was a puddle by his door. An attempt to jump over it failed.

Samuel was leaning on the car.

How young he is, thought Bene. And how little you know about him. He admitted to himself that he loved this man – in a way that was shifting from desire and possession to something else.

He draped Samuel's coat around his shoulders. Wondered what to say. And because Samuel remained stubbornly silent, but could not be persuaded to get back in, Bene told him what he'd been reading. He had found a volume of poetry by Emily Dickinson in the footwell; it must have been there for years. Every book had its time. Reading it too soon was foolish, reading it too late fruitless. One poem captured the song of a bird. The tune was in the tree, the sceptic claimed. Poetry said: it is in you. The ear clothed what it heard in colours both light and dark, and Bene suspected that was true of everything.

They stood like that for a long time. No other cars passed. The sun vanished behind clouds, and when they got back in, Bene didn't even try to step over the puddle.

It's the same for you, he told himself. You drove nearly two thousand kilometres to avoid it. For all time, when he read Dickinson, he would remember this country road. He would remember Samuel, the earthy colours of the plain and the feeling that, despite a lengthy detour, he was exactly where he needed to be.

The village streets were deserted. Everything looked as it always had. And was not the same. Bene noticed derelict buildings, others unrepaired, flaking paint. He remembered the church, its slim spire, the ochre walls, and the green gate of the pastor's house – the rest of the street was unfamiliar, and he wondered what Samuel was feeling as he saw it all again.

Now they had passed the church, pulled up at the gate.

Now they were here.

They stayed in the car until the gate opened.

Out walked a man with a full grey and white beard. He was wearing a brown suit and slippers, as if he'd left the house in a great hurry. Samuel got out of the car so quickly that at first, Bene hesitated to follow.

The two men stood in an embrace that knew no time. Then Hannes came over, and Bene felt the man's strong chest, the top of his belly and his scratchy beard. Hannes' sheer joy at seeing his son again spread to everything. It felt as if Bene was expected too.

Driving into the yard he heard himself praising his Ford, which was filthy from top to bottom. The spark plugs hadn't given him any trouble all the way there. The garden was shabbier, smaller than Bene remembered. The roses had been cut back, the fruit trees were bare. His memories of this place were summer memories, rose beds, grapevines, fruit trees, the scent of honeysuckle – and down by the well, him and Lothar.

First, he noticed the birds.

A surge of many wings.

After sitting for so long in the monotonous engine noise, the air and the soft chorus of chirping carried him into a moment of pure clarity. The closest bushes and trees were dark, almost black; further away, they became light bronze. Behind the last row of trees lay a brightness, as if the world beyond was fading out. Leaves rustled, birds took wing. A sound of absolute presentness. Then he saw a woman. Thin, almost gaunt, in a dark blue coat, headscarf knotted behind. Her face determined and uncompromising, as it had always been. It was a narrow face, covered in freckles and hardly aged, just as her eyes had not aged. They were hard to describe – slightly sunken, with a lot of space between lids and brows.

Florentine was scattering sunflower seeds for the sparrows. In the middle of the movement, she paused. Her hand opened and the bowl fell without making a noise.

Samuel did not move.

Florentine stood still.

Then she spread her arms.

Samuel walked towards his mother's open arms.

And, behind this picture, sparrows swooped on the sunflower seeds.

The kitchen looked exactly as Bene remembered it. The oilcloth covering the table could easily have been the same one.

Hannes did not leave his son's side. Bene blushed under the man's gaze. You brought him back to us, he seemed to be saying. And Bene thought, I am here so I don't have to be elsewhere. It's that simple.

After lunch, they brought the packages in from the car: preserved meat, pasta, bread, sugar, matches, shampoo, soap, cans of beer, cigarettes. Visitors came and went. The gardener Ovidiu slapped Samuel on the back, crying out, 'par avion!' over and over. Samuel's escape must have caused a sensation, and only now did Bene learn the details. The bellringer Rositante covered the pair of them in wet kisses. When she heard that Bene came from northern Germany, she told him she had a brother in Hamburg. Did Bene know him? Some of the things they had brought were given to visitors who, Florentine suspected, would tell the whole village that Samuel was back.

Hannes caught Samuel's eye as he kept glancing at the door.

'Paul went to live with his daughter in Reşiţa.'

Bene didn't know what to make of this sentence, and saw to his surprise that Florentine's eyes had filled with tears.

'I couldn't save him,' said Samuel.

'No one could.'

Florentine came to stand behind her son. Samuel leaned his head back, closed his eyes.

'At least you tried,' she said, softly.

Bene pretended to have left something in the car. His chair scraped across the floor, floorboards creaked, the door swung shut – and he could feel that all these sounds were lifting a spell, that they might call up something that was not to be named. Outside, he let out a breath and sat on the edge of the well.

That evening, the radio told them about the first rulings by the transitional government and the occasional exchange of fire still happening in Bucharest. To the question of who was behind the overthrow, Hannes said that the Securitate stood to profit most from a free market economy, with all that money they had and couldn't spend. The overthrow must have been planned in advance. How else could you explain that there were already oranges in the country for Christmas?

When Florentine went to start the washing up, Bene took the dishcloth from her hand.

'I'll do that – later.'

'You haven't changed,' she said with a smile, and took a cigarette out to the back steps.

Some people spoke first and then reflected – as if their words had to be out in the world to hold up a mirror. Some didn't ask a single question all evening, and others were relentless in their questioning in order to keep the conversation at arm's length. Some people argued with you while others agreed, and only a few, like Florentine and Hannes, possessed an openness that did not need to judge.

One night in the pastor's house revealed this to Bene: everything in the world would return, nothing could be left behind. He could not lock up time in books, for it lived on in him. This kitchen did, and the well in the garden – and there was nothing terrible about longing to go back to the places that had shaped you. Not to confirm those convictions you had already formed, but to show you how in the interim you had become someone else.

Samuel came into the kitchen. Sleepy, in a pair of his father's pyjamas, having brought no nightclothes with him. Florentine poured him a cup of coffee. They leaned on the sink, Florentine in her housecoat, Samuel in pyjamas, and when Hannes joined them dressed as if for an official appointment, it made them both laugh.

Florentine kissed Hannes on the cheek.

Then she looked expectantly at him.

'There's someone else who has been waiting for you,' said Hannes.

'I wrote to her,' said Samuel. 'She never answered.'

'There is an answer you don't yet know.'

They heard footsteps in the hall.

It seemed an eternity before the knock at the door.

'Come in,' said Florentine, without taking her eyes off her son.

Samuel froze. In his stillness, he seemed to be no more than a hand and a coffee cup – just a single hand holding a cup.

A slight woman in a sheepskin coat stood in the doorway. She straightened up and looked Samuel in the eye, with a trace of love, a trace of mistrust, a trace of hurt.

'Sana,' said Samuel.

She was holding the hand of a little girl.

# Prestigio

· · · · ·

A story can be told so often and so vividly that you think you remember it yourself. Some stories are told so many times that contexts are refreshed and previously unknown interpretations emerge – and with each re-telling they steadily, imperceptibly change. Details are added, others left out. Along the way uncertainty increases, and something can move ever further away until it is entirely forgotten. Another aspect can become ever sharper, until you're seeing it through clear glass.

The step Livia took was one of these stories.

It was one of those days when the summer was dwindling away. There were many of these, sometimes they went on for weeks, and only in hindsight would you be able to say: yes, that was the day when summer started to feel remote and stale. The leaves dry, the grass downtrodden, something clandestine about the bushes. What had once been warmth and light began to harden, no longer blazed, became the foretaste of farewell. And just as you can leave something behind but never quite let go of it, all at once you know it is too late for summer dreams.

The lake was dammed on one side, and stretched between wooded hills and a road. A ferry called every two hours. At the boat-hire place they chose a pedalo. Livia's mother took a seat with her and Jarik on the rear sun deck. Her father sat at the pedals with Livia's godfather. The water was almost black. It had a restless movement to it that provoked a kind of tension in Livia's mother, something too faint to call a premonition.

A blanket was spread out; the two men came to join the others. The boat bobbed on the water, waves slapped the hull, a wilful, warning rhythm. The plastic was chapped, almost like tree bark. A low railing ran around the sides but the back of the boat was open, with a ladder leading down into the water. No one wanted to swim that day.

Liv was three years old. She knew the difference between dry land and water. And yet she stood up, walked purposefully towards the back, and kept going when the boat ended. The expression on her face never changed, her mother liked to say. She'd been fooled by her daughter's expression, it was neither playful nor cocky, and that made her untouchable, superior and, in some odd way, protected. When Liv stood up, no one was alarmed. They were all drowsy from the sun, which shone dully in a washed-out sky streaked with haze – and they watched as Liv, carefree, blessed, took one step out beyond the boat.

The lake swallowed her.

The men leapt up. Her father was the quickest to act. He leaned over the edge and with one determined arm pulled Liv back up. She didn't scream, didn't thrash about, simply reached a hand upwards, and her father swiftly found this hand in the blackness of the lake.

It was over as quickly as it had begun.

Liv did not cry. Only the look on her mother's face made her realise something was wrong. Her father fell to his knees;

her mother took her in her arms. Without further ado, they went back to shore. Her godfather carried her to the car, the blanket a cloak flapping around her shoulders. Her father drove fast, eager to distance them from the lake, as if what had happened there might catch up with them.

The story was often told ('Remember when Liv…?') at parties, birthdays, and always near water. What had moved her parents about the incident was the casual way Liv stepped out onto the lake. It hadn't mattered to her whether it was water or land, and in that carefree moment she had mistaken death for life.

Liv had heard the story so often that she seemed to remember the details. The rough plastic skin, the dull slapping against the rump of the pedalo, the sensation of sinking, the painful jerk in her arm as her father pulled her out. Though many years had passed, she had the feeling that her father remained watchful, fearing she would take a heedless step. A step over the edge.

Liv went to the bistro on the corner.

She cast a hasty glance at her reflection in the windowpane, dark shadows around her eyes, chin-length, wavy hair. She tucked the hair behind her ear, pushed up the sleeves of her jacket (for a while now she had been wearing men's clothes, bought by the kilo from a second-hand shop) and hoped she looked serene as she walked through the door. She studied the menu, checked the lunchtime special pretending she couldn't make up her mind, though the meaning of the letters barely registered. His eyes rested on her like a coiled spring, frank, piercing – say something, Liv told herself, picking some random dish from the menu, to take away, because when he was there, there was nowhere to hide and no place to flee.

Recently, the boy from the bistro had helped Liv pump up her bike tyre. He'd asked if she needed help, he'd probably been watching from the restaurant for a while, and she stepped aside in the absurd hope that he, too, would fail. When he knelt down by the rear tyre to check the valve, she noticed a Japanese character on the back of his neck. He brushed a hand across his face. It left a dark smear on his cheek and by the time the tyre had been inflated, Liv couldn't utter a coherent sentence.

On the other hand, perhaps 'thank you' was a full sentence.

Since then, he smiled and looked at her differently. He handed her the food with emphasis, holding the bowl longer, counting the change more slowly, as if trying to delay her departure. Familiarity came with strangeness, the two always together. The strangeness sat deeper; both uncertainty and shame arose solely because of her presence, the knowledge that your life touched that of others, and that this was actually going on all the time.

Liv sat on the wall outside school, calling to mind every word he'd said, and when Anna came to sit beside her and asked what she had eaten, she couldn't remember right away. While Liv felt safe only when observing others from a distance, her friend connected with people quickly. They would never have become friends if Anna hadn't spoken to Liv first.

'Where are you from?' she'd asked.

Liv had launched into a detailed explanation, assuming Anna meant her background, until she realised that the girl from the parallel class was only asking where she lived.

Later, Anna said she had noticed Liv staring at her. Liv disputed that, though she probably had stared – being fascinated by Anna's self-confidence; by the natural way she greeted the others, or didn't, but always held their attention; by the light hair falling loose over her shoulders – imagining that she was doing it discreetly.

In summer, they had flown to Corfu together. It was their first holiday without parents, and they had worked four stultifying weeks on a supermarket checkout to pay for it. On the island, they hired mopeds and rode along the coast. Liv was a good driver, but on one stretch she misjudged the bends and scraped against the rocks edging the road. A woman in the nearest village cleaned the grazes with disinfectant. Built upon a slope, one house stood a little apart; it was whitewashed with blue shutters. Liv said she had never seen a more beautiful house, and they learned that it belonged to a man whose wife had died in a sailing accident. Someone whom the water called but did not release, thought Liv. They rode on, though Liv's knees were trembling. She felt the wind on her wounds and knew: you have to do this now, or you'll never get back on.

One night, their route home from a taverna took them through the same village. It was raining, a fine, misty rain, soft on the skin – blessed rain, someone called it.

Liv signalled to Anna to pull over. A silhouette stood on the terrace of the house, a man leaning on the balustrade, looking out at the water. Loud music blared from open windows above the village, the sound drifting out to sea. Liv sensed the man's loneliness, as if for that moment she was hugging him. Anna pressed her to keep going. They rode on through the night, the roads glistening, the rain falling gently, the waves surging against the coast; everything was filled with life, and she was nothing but a small, moving dot.

Remembering this incident, it seemed to her that this was the distance needed in order to see someone. As you came closer things grew more uncertain, and began to blur.

The school bell rang.

'Another two hours of maths,' said Anna, drawing out the words.

Liv took the deck of cards from inside her jacket, split them in half and riffled them together along the short sides. The cards slotted precisely one into another, like a zip.

'If I shuffle the cards like that eight times, the deck will be in the same order it was to begin with. That works with 52 cards; with 64, you would only need six shuffles. Plus, I can keep tabs on any card. That's maths.'

Anna laughed, and Liv held the cards up to her face in two fans, so only her eyes were showing.

When she left school in the late afternoon, the boy from the bistro was rewriting the pavement sign. Their eyes met, and Liv weighed up the possibility of having lunch elsewhere in future.

The warmth had vanished with the setting sun. The cloudless blue sky deepened the darkness in the streets. Liv climbed the steps of the opera house, entered the oval rotunda and went into a toilet. She freshened her deodorant and put on a bowtie, a flea-market find that she had smuggled into the house, since her mother did not share her new passion for second-hand clothes.

Tonight's performance was *Norma*. Liv felt the slight tension that always set in when the house was fully lit, but still empty. Marie-Luise was the only other person already there. Malu, who had worked there longest, had a boyish face with wide-set eyes. She wore glasses on a cord and always dressed in black. She pressed Liv to her, then held her at arm's length and eyed the bowtie approvingly.

'You're beautiful,' said Malu. Before Liv could reply, she handed her the little bag of change and sent her to the middle section of the cloakroom, where in her experience it would be busiest. And it was. Liv hung up jackets and coats, knotted scarves to sleeves, stowed umbrellas and rucksacks and handed out the tokens, aware of what was happening to either side, checking all was well. When the performance began, she sat down on a chair between the coat racks. Malu met latecomers, took them to the doormen, who decided whether they could be let in or had to wait for the interval, lined up the rucksacks neatly and then leaned (this being the most slack she would cut herself) against the counter.

Liv liked the cloakroom smell of perfume and mothballs, the building's grey, silver and gold tones, the intense activity when everything began, the audience members' dressy clothes, the time during the performance when things were mostly quiet, the hubbub of voices in the interval, the applause and the bustle when coats, jackets, scarves and rucksacks found their owners again amid the crush.

When the show had been running half an hour, Malu sent her in. Liv went up to the third tier, where the doorman nodded to her and quietly opened the door. She found an empty seat in the back row. It was hard to concentrate on the music; her mind drifted to the singers' costumes, which looked like something from the Godfather films, and to who would present the bouquets that evening – a task which no one really liked and which always fell to one of the cloakroom ladies.

Liv noticed an older man on the other side of the aisle. He sat up straight, not leaning on the back of his seat, and held his hat in both hands. The man reminded her of her great-grandfather. Perhaps because he looked as lost as Johann had, whether sitting on the train or at the kitchen table or asleep in his armchair. He had existed at Karlina's side, a person who was tolerated, though no one could say what kind of tolerance that took. He contented himself with turning up for meals and otherwise read the paper in the living room or watched television. Twice a week he dressed himself carefully, put on a hat and strolled along Königstraße. Liv's father, who sometimes accompanied him, said he had the impression that in his mind, Johann was walking down the boulevard back in Hermannstadt, sitting on a bench there with the other men who read the paper in silence and played chess – and Liv remembered the men in the city park, knitted waistcoats over shirts and cigarettes in the corner of their mouths, faces tired, but inquisitive and wily, too.

While Johann was still alive, the family would be invited for lunch on the first Sunday of the month. Karlina and Johann lived in one of the many cube-like apartment blocks on the city's outskirts. Their flat was on the fifth floor, and its front door led straight into the dining room, with the kitchen leading off it. A windowless hallway turned a right-hand corner round to the living room and bedroom. A third room, the one Liv found most exciting, contained provisions, spare crockery, a fold-out guest bed. Johann never seemed to know what to talk about to her and her brother Jarik, but he saved all the newspapers and magazines, and when Karlina poured nut liqueur after the meal, he would sit down with Liv and encourage her to cut out interesting articles.

Once, Liv had run away from home. She had argued with her mother, and this time even her father, who always stood by her (keeping quiet about her getting home late, defending her school grades as adequate) had taken her mother's side. Liv ran right out of the house, with no coat, no money. She rode the escalators in a department store, searched the lockers at the museum for forgotten coins, put her feet in a fountain. By the evening, it became clear that the idea of bolting was more audacious than the reality. Without a ticket, she boarded a tram from the central station, rode to the end of the line and rang her great-grandparents' doorbell. Johann was sitting in the living room, looking at newspapers. I'm glad you're here, was all Karlina said. She made semolina pudding, then took Liv into the bedroom where a clock ticked so loudly that moving time forwards seemed full of effort, and covered her with a particularly beautiful and particularly soft quilt.

When Liv woke, her father was sitting at the bedside, looking at her as if he hadn't seen her for a long time.

Liv went out just before the interval. The man in the back row nodded to her, and she nodded too – amicably, as if they had met here on purpose.

The light on the staircase suddenly seemed glaring, and she wished she was back in the auditorium. Her mind turned to the newspaper cuttings she had saved in a folder but never read, to Karlina, who checked the sky for clouds every morning (clear days were the ones she couldn't bear), to the boy from the bistro who passed her food with one arm outstretched, the other bent behind his back.

Malu saw how things were right away and wrapped her arms around her.

'Casta Diva,' she said, as soberly as a doctor giving a diagnosis. 'I wanted you to hear it.'

Liv didn't know what it was she had heard, just that she had lost herself somewhere between memory and the present, and that giving people the right coat now seemed impossible.

After the interval, Malu asked for a magic trick.

The cloakroom ladies and two doormen gathered at the counter. Liv stood on the other side, tucked her hair behind her ear and began to tell her story. Her godfather Bene had taught her that storytelling was part of the distraction, perhaps even the real art. Seven years ago when he gave her a magic box – because to his regret she was not much of a reader – no one could have guessed what he had started, Liv least of all.

Every magician had a least favourite card, said Liv as she shuffled. For her it was the king of spades, the ruler with the upturned black heart. In French, the suit was called piques, meaning pikes. A pike was given to an enlisted soldier without gun or horse. It was the most basic of weapons; that was where the expression 'plain as a pikestaff' came from. Liv fanned out the cards and asked Malu to pick one, warning her that it must not be the king of spades under any circumstances. Malu took her time, running her fingers over the fan, pausing, moving a few cards further on and pulling out – the king of spades. The audience laughed. Liv showed them that it was a normal pack of 52 playing cards. Then she slipped the king of spades back into the deck, shuffled and split it, flicking the cards from one hand to the other until Malu said stop. The king of spades, again. No matter how many times Liv let Malu choose, she could not pick a different card.

'I think you should keep him. The king wants to be with you.'

Malu put the card away and said it would bring her luck.

Then Liv held out the cards to one of the doormen. He drew the five of diamonds. Liv asked him to write his name on it. She put the card back into the middle of the deck, slowly, in front of everyone, snapped her fingers, and now the signed diamond lay on top. The doorman was taken aback, and Liv received a spontaneous round of applause. Watch very closely, said Liv, and repeated the miracle. The audience relied on their eyes. But the eyes were the easiest to deceive.

First, magic was a craft.

Then it was entertainment.

But really, it was deception.

To deceive people convincingly, they had to be watching your hands. It came down to the smallest of movements. A magician had to know what the audience saw, which is why you practised in front of the mirror until you could perform a sequence straight through. Pauses, hesitation, uncertainty destroyed a performance. This was discouraging to begin with, but Bene said that with time and a great deal of practice, it would become improbably easy to pull the wool over the audience's eyes.

How did he know that? He wasn't a magician.

He just knew it, he said.

If a magician came to town, Liv would sit right at the front so she could see their face and hands. You learned by copying, but you didn't just steal someone's tricks; you translated them into something new.

Every magic trick consisted of three acts. The magician introduced an idea, showed you something, then made it disappear. The trick only succeeded when the thing was made to reappear. This act was the most difficult; it always held the possibility of failure but it was all-important. Prestigio – the finale.

Only the end reveals how successful the beginning has been.


When Liv got home that evening, only Jarik was there. His door was closed, but she could hear he was still awake.

She went into the kitchen, where her mother had left supper, with a note that said, 'Microwave, four minutes'.

Stana was the only mother in Liv's circle of friends with a full-time job. She had carried on studying architecture after Jarik was born, and set up her own practice with friends when she finished. If anyone implied that Liv and her brother were being neglected, Samuel would say that in the end children brought themselves up. Admittedly, that worked better in the Banat than in a city in Baden-Württemberg.

Her mother's desk had once stood in the hallway; now she had her own study. Stana didn't subscribe to the theory that adults didn't need a room of their own. Her rules were: everyone needed their own room, and furniture had to be chosen with the utmost care and never purchased from one of the huge furniture stores they had here. Stana had a horror of livingroom wall units with all their compartments, and wardrobes with sliding doors. A sliding door was the gateway to hell, she liked to say. Just looking at those wall units would do lasting psychological damage – why weren't people warned?

Everything that came into the house had to pass a test. You couldn't buy a thing just because it existed. The elements that made up their home had to be protected, and after any argument she opened the windows and let in the wind.

Liv's father, meanwhile, had no fixed profession. He had been several things: fishmonger, taxi driver, caretaker, doorman at the circus, cable-puller on a late-night show, bus driver, forestry worker. According to him, he could do everything and nothing, and once you had made your peace with that, it was enough. Liv's mother had her own theory for why Samuel never stayed anywhere very long. When he'd worked as a caretaker, she had noticed people roping him into pointless tasks because they wanted to be near him. There was something about him, a calm or presence that people longed for, and even though (or perhaps because) he didn't talk much, he was held to be a good conversationalist. Long term, business suffered. Someone was always badmouthing him, telling tales, showing him the door. He had strayed from what people called a career path, but there was pleasure in success and freedom in surrender, said Samuel.

Liv had only recently realised how women saw her father. Her own friends fell silent in his presence or talked too much; though with other mothers and fathers her visitors tried to get the pleasantries over as quickly as possible, they spent a noticeably long time talking to her parents and seeming to enjoy it. Anna thought Samuel good-looking. Liv disagreed; he was young compared to other parents, that was all.

Liv didn't know which was better: to have a fixed profession or to be everything and nothing. But she knew it was good to complete each other. Her parents' story was a crazy one: her father had fled the country overnight and her birth was kept secret so he wouldn't return and risk being sent to prison. Trust had needed time to reestablish itself, but there had never been any serious doubt that her parents belonged together.

Some days they all pottered around the house, each in their own world, until hunger brought them to the kitchen – where her parents made food while she and Jarik talked. In the evening they all lounged on the sofa, her mother beside Jarik, Liv beside her father, legs stretched out on the coffee table. The light of the television shivered through the room, and it didn't matter what was on; nothing was more important than this closeness.

As the microwave pinged, footsteps came up the stairs: the energetic tread of her mother, her father's muted step. A bunch of keys jangled into the bowl, coats were draped over the banisters. Liv took her reheated food into the living room. She said something, talking the whole way from the kitchen; later she couldn't remember what about. Then she saw her father. He was sitting on the sofa with his face in his hands. The room was dark, the only light coming from the hall.

'What's wrong?' asked Liv.

Stana stood in the doorway. Behind her, Jarik appeared in his pyjamas.

'Karlina has died,' said Samuel. And although he said it very quietly, Liv was sure Jarik, too, had heard from the stairs, that the whole street knew and every last person in this city paused for a moment.

Liv's father didn't seem to notice that the living room light was off, that Stana had folded Jarik in her arms and Liv was still standing there, the plate in her hands.

'What colour is sadness?' Samuel had asked once, one summer in the Banat when Liv had refused to go home. She had climbed onto the shed roof and announced that she was staying here, they could send her parcels from Germany.

'Midnight blue.'

'Where does it start?'

'Here,' said Liv, and she had laid her hands on her chest.

Eventually he had asked if sadness had a name.

And she had said the name of the sadness.

Her father had advised her to pay attention to everything, not to push it away, and Liv felt overflowing heaviness, the pounding of her heart, the warmth of the shed roof, a splinter in her palm, then, hesitantly, a spreading, swelling calm that had allowed her to come down off the roof and – once Florentine had removed the splinter with tweezers – to get into the car.

Liv's hands began to pulse, her arms grew heavy. She put down the plate and sat beside her father. Did his sadness have a name?

Karlina had survived Johann by a year.

After a fall, she had gone into hospital and then into a care home. Karlina never spoke a word to the woman she shared a room with. She was dissatisfied with the carers and barely touched the food. It was not possible, she said, for her to sit at a table in the presence of strangers and wait for a plastic tray to be set in front of her, and when Liv cast a glance into the dining room from the wide corridor smelling of apples and disinfectant, she understood what her great-grandmother meant.

The family took it in turns to keep Karlina company and bring food. Others might regret that little remained of a life's worth of things; Karlina didn't. The things that had been most important to her, seagull house and weathercock, were long gone. She asked only for the sheepskin that had always lain on her bed, and a picture of the king. Not so long ago, King Michael had retaken ownership of his palaces in Romania, thereby indirectly renouncing the throne. Karlina, the ardent monarchist, had found it hard to forgive him for that.

When she had visitors, she handed over shopping lists that were more or less sensible: acacia honey, washing soda, portions of coffee cream. Despite her highly developed sense of style, in Germany Karlina only shopped at the Norma discount supermarkets. If something wasn't there, if honey had sold out, for instance, then she would wait until 'Frau Norma' had it again. It was as impossible to talk Karlina out of this as it was to wean her off Kraft Singles. She liked the cheese at the cheese counter, but it was too expensive. She would not abandon certain notions: that Schwarzkopf shampoo was only for dark-haired people, that frozen food would be the end of her.

In one of her last phone calls, she had claimed that a burglar was lying under her bed. They had gone to the care home, where they found Karlina composed and dressed as if for important visitors. Stana served up the food they had brought, and Karlina ate in silence, a linen napkin on her lap, taking care not to spill or rest her elbows on the table. In her view, a person's character was to be judged by their table manners, which amounted to a scathing verdict on Liv and her brother.

Samuel asked if the burglar had gone.

'Can't you see him? He's been under the bed all this time, watching us,' Karlina replied. There was no fear in her voice; this was merely an observation, sober and with a hint of surprise that others were incapable of seeing the obvious.

Liv's parents went out to speak to one of the carers. Liv chatted to her great-grandmother, mostly listening, wanting to see where her thoughts led her.

At some point Karlina asked why Jarik's trousers were ripped.

Jarik looked down at his legs and said that was the latest thing.

'Here, one person puts on ripped trousers, and then everyone puts on ripped trousers, can the pair of you explain that to me?'

Karlina was given medication that put her in a twilight state, interspersed with hours of rebellion when she wanted to see Hannes, him, only him, none of her other sons, the traitors who had put her away in here. If her two sisters came to visit, she would ask why Emma wasn't with them. Then came periods of that calm and serenity that were her defining feature, a self-containment that did not need anyone or anything.

Karlina had always had the gift of stealing away without anyone knowing where she was going.

Florentine and Hannes travelled over for the funeral. Malva came without Konstanty. This was treated like a novelty (I'm afraid your grandfather can't make it this time), though everyone knew that he and Stana had decided it between them.

An air of foreignness surrounded Liv's grandparents. Scarcely perceptible when she was lying on the rug with Hannes, listening to the Beatles – for Hannes, *The White Album* was the best, and for Liv it was *Rubber Soul* – or smoking in secret with Florentine in the loggia, or watching television with Malva. But on the street, in shops, in the presence of friends, there was a stiffness, almost an embarrassment, that set them apart from others. Their clothes, too, knitted waistcoats and headscarves, and their language, always slightly deviating from standard German. An overcoat was a mantle, the fridge was an ice box, snacks were leaveners. Florentine said, 'spake' instead of 'spoke', and 'Samuel's kin,' which included them all. As Malva spoke no German and Hannes no Slovakian, the adults talked in Romanian, which Liv and Jarik didn't understand. While they were all visiting, three languages took turns.

In the Banat, nobody felt foreign, and Liv thought that perhaps everyone had a place where they belonged. Some people had to go away to find it, and others would never find it if they left.

'A shepherd stays with his flock,' said Hannes, though almost all the Germans in the village had emigrated. Florentine couldn't imagine abandoning her garden, and the West held no allure for Konstanty. Why Malva didn't leave, even though her daughter urged her to, saying she could come and live with them, no one knew. Only Karlina and Johann had emigrated, one year after the revolution. They had settled near their two other sons in southwest Germany. And because Stana wanted to study and Samuel could no longer bear the sight of the sea, the family made the decision to settle in the same place.

Liv's godfather arrived from the North Sea, bringing Lorenzo with him.

Bene made an effort to seem matter-of-fact. Kept a distance, kept detaching his eyes, his hands from his boyfriend, and in this self-imposed restraint Liv saw the magnitude of his affection. A magician gathers all the information she can. Liv began making mental notes. How did he move, what did he talk about, what were his interests? She liked Lorenzo. Anyone who dared to meet the extended family at a funeral had to have guts.

When they entered the chapel where Karlina was laid out, Liv noticed it at once. She told Florentine, who was checking the candles weren't too close to the flowers, and then everyone saw.

Hannes rounded on the people from the funeral director's, asked if they had lost their minds; where had his mother's clothes come from? His brothers had to stop him taking off her blouse in front of the assembled mourners. Karlina hated buttons. And now she was lying there in a skirt and blouse with a long row of gleaming, mother-of-pearl buttons. Someone changed her out of them – her clothes had been mixed up with those of another dead woman.

At the funeral repast, Liv sat next to Malva. Her grandmother had grey, curly hair that escaped stubbornly from the knot at the back of her head. She laid her hands on the table, outstretched, resigned, as if to say: take them and do with them what you will. The sight of the proffered hands unsettled Liv. She held them, and Malva returned the pressure, with some delay and no conviction.

Bene told the story of how he'd met Karlina. He had returned to Romania with Samuel the summer after the wall came down, flying direct to Hermannstadt.

'Lina opened the gate and said we were right on time. Although we were a week early because, as it turned out, Samuel had given her the wrong arrival date.'

'Such beauty should be shared out between several men, she said when she saw you,' Samuel added.

To distract from his blushes, Bene asked about the picture of the king.

'Which king?' said Lorenzo.

Samuel offered to let Bene have the picture, and although Bene's delight was obvious, he hesitated to accept the gift.

'It will have a good home with you,' Samuel assured him.

The two men looked at each other. Lorenzo, his question still unanswered, turned his full attention to the dessert.

Karlina was gone, thought Liv, and so many stories with her. Her parents held the memory of her grandparents, her grandparents the memory of her great-grandparents. That was how it worked.

Samuel's arm lay along the back of Stana's chair. When Liv's mother leaned back, he picked up the movement. It seemed to

Liv that he would always wait for her, come to meet her, always be halfway there.

The lower compartment of her mother's jewellery box held a note. A tattered, worn note in her father's handwriting. The letters were formed carefully, as if he'd had to coax each individual letter to appear.

*Forgive me. Do not wait for me. I am never gone from you. S.*

Of all possible words of farewell, her mother had had to content herself with these. They were not a promise, conveyed no hope, no sense of any future, swore no oaths, didn't even explain. When Liv was a child, Stana had told her that a dragon made her father flee. She had never questioned it. All the same, thought Liv, he could have stayed.

Through the window, Liv watched Jarik drawing lines in the gravel with the toe of his shoe, while Hannes asked the staff for a ball and followed him outside, and Florentine tidied Malva's hair. She saw Bene pretending to straighten the tablecloth, but really watching Lorenzo, who was chatting to Auguste and Marie. She heard her mother whisper something to her father, and wondered what she really knew about these people. And if she knew nothing, then neither did the others, and instead of a long line of memories there was just a continual vanishing and forgetting, until platitudes were all that remained from these events, no real knowledge, just interpretations passed down. A whole life in all its contradictions could be summarised in a few sentences.

The thing that vanished had to reappear. And who but a magician could ensure that things were not lost?

Anna had decided that Liv needed to get out of the house. She couldn't spend the whole weekend indoors, staring at the ceiling. Someone had tickets for a gig in Munich. Liv wanted nothing more than to lie on the bed and stare at the ceiling until her thoughts dissolved and time itself dwindled to uncountable tininess. All the same, she said yes.

Liv sat with Anna in the back. Marko was at the wheel, Tim in the passenger seat. There was one more person to collect.

It's going to be a squeeze, thought Liv.

The door opened, and although at first there was not much to see, she recognised his voice even before he leaned down and asked her to move over.

Noah – the boy from the bistro.

Liv could never remember names right away. Most fell straight through her, very few snagged and stayed, and nothing was more embarrassing than being addressed by name when the other person remained nameless, and only quick thinking would save her from being exposed. Names and people often didn't connect; it wasn't her fault, but that of the person who had not managed to attach themselves to their name. Only later, when they had left the city, did it occur to Liv that she had forgotten to introduce herself.

'Slow down,' said Tim, after a bend where cigarette papers, tobacco and weed almost slid off the car user manual. On the motorway, he turned up the music and lit the joint. Massive Attack was playing. Marko's VW only had speakers in the front, but it didn't matter, they knew the album off by heart. Marko was one of those people who talked and forgot to pass it on. Anna tapped him on the shoulder. Liv took her time, had two drags, passed it on. Noah – Liv liked the sound of the vowels in the middle – declined. For the first few kilometres she had tried not to get too close to him, but eventually she gave up, accepting that the whole right side of her body was leaning against his left.

It began to snow. Lane markers passed under the car like a conveyor belt. Liv stared straight ahead. Noah wound down the window. It grew cold. He wound the window back up, glanced at Liv, and Liv took in his calmness, which was like something approaching from a long way off.

When they had found the venue in Munich, they wondered at the empty carpark. Then they spotted the poster: concert postponed due to illness.

For a minute everyone talked over one another, and then it was silent.

'What do we do, now we're here?' Anna asked.

They couldn't agree, and the discussion ended with them deciding to drive back. Noah waited until everyone was in the car, and then sat next to Liv again.

There wasn't much traffic on the A8. The snow was heavier now.

Marko kept to the right-hand lane. Thick, watery snow-flakes flew at the windscreen. The wipers seemed to be out of synch; the music was turned down low. They stared at the flurries, lane markings barely visible now. Everyone was driving slowly; they could look into other cars like boats gliding by. Marko shuffled forward in his seat. He was the only one with a licence, so no one could take over. Eventually he indicated and pulled into a petrol station. Although he let the VW roll slowly in, it still careened, sliding towards some rubbish skips, bumping them lightly before stopping. The slide had played out like a silent film. Not even Anna, who could be quite loud, had panicked.

Marko said he couldn't keep driving.

'But we can't stay here, either,' said Tim.

As soon as the engine was off, the cold gripped.

'Let's go inside,' Noah suggested.

A brightly lit petrol station surrounded by snow-covered trees. The chill of snowflakes on skin – Liv stopped and raised her face. She paid attention to the snow as it fell on roads, trees, cars, people, to the brightness and the darkness behind it. Nothing, she thought, could be so beautiful and so threatening at once.

'Come on!' Anna called out.

There were few people in the petrol station. The man behind the counter eyed them. They strolled along the rows of shelves, bought crisps, chocolate, something to drink. Noah, who had stayed apart from the others, beckoned them over. He had found a baby changing room. Tim tapped his forehead at him, but when he saw that everyone was following Noah, he did too.

The room had a toilet and a shower as well as the changing table, but the crucial item was the radiator. Marko slid his back down it and closed his eyes. Tim sat in the shower and opened a bag of crisps. Anna climbed onto the changing table and curled into a ball, which no one else could have done. The silence set them apart from one another. Liv saw a flash of the Japanese character on the back of Noah's neck as he locked the door; she stood indecisively in the room for a while and then sat beside him. Glanced at him from time to time, closed her eyes, stretched out her legs, noticed that Noah was stretching his legs out, too, lowering his arm, his fingers touching hers. Nothing was chance and yet it was inevitable. In the night, Liv's head slid onto Noah's shoulder, and he held her hand in his.

On waking, there was no time to think about heads and hands seeking each other out. They were jolted awake by Tim's shrieks. Marko had turned the shower on over him and was helpless with laughter. Anna snapped at him, then helped Tim dry his clothes under the hand dryer.

Liv and Noah went to get coffee.

The woman at the till watched in astonishment as they appeared from the corridor leading to the toilets, but asked no questions.

'I heard you do magic tricks,' said Noah.

Liv told him to look in his breast pocket.

Noah's hand travelled slowly to his chest, though his eyes never left her. He pulled a paper bird out of his coat. Wings, tail feathers, head, all folded out of his gig ticket.

'How did you know I like origami?'

He turned the bird over in his hands.

Liv turned to the coffee machine, hiding her smile.

They drank coffee from plastic cups and drove back on gritted roads. It soon became clear this was a story that would be told often.

Beginnings had to be decided upon; endings arrived on their own, without you deciding.

There was a beginning with Noah. A beginning with walks and talks, with closeness that grew slowly. They browsed second-hand bookshops and antique stores, tried on hats in a hat shop, admired expensive cigars in a tobacconist, sat in cafés and watched the customers at other tables. A homeless man begged, passers-by thronged under the arcades, a dog escaped its owner, and Liv had the urge to know what it was, this thing between her and Noah.

Noah often helped in his parents' bistro. Sometimes Liv went there to eat when she wasn't hungry. She wanted to watch him fill her plate, one arm behind his back, one outstretched, always ensuring he touched Liv casually as he served her. His mother, who took the money, was friendly, but didn't show too much interest. You're not the first, thought Liv, and to her surprise felt an aversion to the fact.

At the weekend, he picked her up from work. He waited until the last coat had been collected, the takings counted. Malu asked Noah so many questions it made Liv uncomfortable.

'You had to go through it, he has to go through it,' she said.

And Liv hoped that Noah would pass muster with Malu.

On the tram, they played a game. Each had to reveal a thought they had never spoken aloud. Liv admitted that she felt sorry for the little strips of land imprisoned between the tramlines. They had no purpose, no one noticed them, they were a kind of leftover.

'I sometimes imagine what it would be like to be someone else,' said Noah. 'Someone coming in the door and seeing me.'

Liv told him about a man who had swum out into the open sea, attached to a rope, to look at his boat from outside when it was in full sail. It was only later that he realised the danger he'd put himself in. But he couldn't bear not being able to see the whole of his boat. The experience of being on it wasn't enough.

'That's exactly what I want. To see myself from outside – I mean, really see myself,' said Noah.

'But you can,' said Liv.

And thought: don't you know this?

'Through the people around you. They all see you, each in their own way. You're not the man coming through the door, but you are the one sitting here and watching the man come through the door. Does that make sense?' she added, because he wasn't saying anything.

'Yes,' said Noah, and kissed her.

Only language desired separation, thought Liv, as they lay on her bed one evening listening to music. In life, one thing merged into another. Always.

She was wearing one of Noah's jumpers. It was dark in the room. When a car passed, everything the headlights touched was transformed into shadows: trees, streetlamps, electricity masts. They came in through the window, slid over the bed, over Noah's face. Liv wished that things were not so deceiving, so transient, faltering, so fleetingly beautiful. She wished there was something reliable, abiding.

All at once, she saw an image of Florentine folding her laundry. She laid edge to edge as she folded, smoothing each item with the palms of her hands and this gesture held everything, appreciation for what wrapped the body alongside the yearning to be the fabric that touched the skin of those you loved. Liv saw her mother swimming in the Marosch, letting herself drift, lying in the leaf-shade of the willows. She had held Liv and Jarik, eyes on the water, eyes on the sky, until they grew brave enough to surrender to the current.

Noah began to caress her neck and shoulders. He rubbed his palms until they were warm and covered her ears. She heard a whispering sound. Then he laid his hands over her eyes. One sense after another vanished and returned. He stroked her hair, a tingling that started in her scalp moved over her body and, when the song ended, Liv pressed repeat.

The plane trees in the palace gardens were bare. The snow had melted. A gentle wind moved down the paths.

Florentine had told her that as a little boy Samuel thought that the wind carried words. Words in other languages, some he had often heard and others whose meaning was slow to reveal itself – and he did not feel called upon to answer. No answer was required. Somewhere people were waiting for words that elsewhere were too much. There was no balance, always a too much and a too little.

Stana was working on a big commission and these days only came home when everyone had gone to bed. In the past, they had often picked Liv's mother up from work. Samuel would get changed, and Liv and Jarik had to put on clean clothes as well. These were standards Karlina had set, which no one questioned to this day. They would go to the Italian place for espresso and ice cream. Stana might have to return to the office afterwards, and over time Liv's father had extended his repertoire of pancake recipes.

Samuel had asked if Liv wanted to come with him. The tiny pause between his question and her answer told them that this ritual might not last much longer.

When they reached the café by the lake, they stopped. The water was dark, only a trace of green along the bank. Liv remembered the incident at the lake and knew her father was thinking about it, too. Her carefree demeanour, the rapid sinking, everything was present to her, because she often still didn't know whether it was water or land.

'Do you have any new year wishes?' Samuel asked.

Liv moved her head from side to side.

A magician was an honest liar.

He seemed content with that. They could walk on, settling into the silence, because they were at home there; silence was where they found each other.

'Before I fled,' said Samuel, whose eyes had taken on the colour of the water, 'I wanted to write your mother a letter. I managed three sentences, that was all. I wrote hundreds, and three were left. They won't have helped her. They didn't help me. You can overestimate love, expect too much of it. Love, more than anything. We could have lost each other. Through freedom, habit, chance, time. So if you have a wish, say it. Don't rely on it coming to you, or staying with you.'

Liv tucked her hair behind her ear, smoothed the fringe of her scarf, untangled the cords of her jacket. If she could have found anything else to straighten, she would have. Her father had never spoken about the letter before, never confided his doubt.

Stana came down the gravel path towards them. She walked quickly, but not hurriedly, avoiding the puddles.

Samuel watched Stana approach. But Liv watched her father.

The audience will always look where the magician is looking. The magician becomes the eyes of the audience.

# THANKS AND ACKNOWLEDGEMENTS

· · · · ·

For information, advice and early readings, I would like to thank Renate, Ralf and Helmut Wolff, Andreas Thies, Julia Knapp, Katja Leuchtenberger, Rico Müller-Schmitt, Uschi and Harro Stefanovici, Günter Wolff, Katharine Leiska, André Gerke, Toni Nachbar, as well as my agent Caterina Schäfer and my editor, Corinna Kroker.

Richard Wagner's poem, Wald, (*Gold: Gedichte*, © Aufbau Verlag, 2017) appears courtesy of Dr Christina Rossi.

## TRANSLATOR'S NOTE

· · · · ·

This short novel encompasses a large world. The history of Romania and of the Banat and its German-speaking population throughout the twentieth century shapes each of the characters' lives. Their everyday is also vividly evoked through food, architecture, customs and landscapes.

Allusions to historical figures, events and cultural phenomena aren't always explained, however. Iris Wolff leaves space for readers to infer and interpret for themselves, and these omissions are complemented by a masterful use of ambiguity and double meanings. All of this challenges the translator. You have to do your research, understand the workings of this submerged world, and ask questions to help unpick those ambiguous phrases. You need to know exactly what is going on – but only in order to recreate the same ambiguity in another language. There's a strong temptation to gloss, to add a few words of context, to hold the reader's hand more than the original does. I have done my best to resist. The poetic elements of Wolff's prose speak for themselves; the rest (history, politics, culture) is for readers to choose to investigate – or not.

*Blurred* uses a scattering of Transylvanian Saxon, a dialect – arguably a language in its own right – from the Moselle-Franconian language family spoken by the German population of Transylvania, which is quite closely related to Luxembourgish. Many words sound archaic to speakers of 'standard' German. For this reason, particularly in the early chapters where dialect is more evident, I have chosen not to substitute fragments of place-based English dialect, but to use words that originate in Old English (e.g. ado, byre), and a few French loanwords (cortège, chaise longue) to reflect the French influence on the language. My intention here is to give a subtle flavour to the text without continually pulling readers out of the novel's world with obscure and unfamiliar terms. One or two particularly resonant Transylvanian Saxon words have however been left as in the original, for the sheer pleasure of them. 'Purligar', for instance, is the term that Karlina uses for the homeless men who live around the station in Sibiu. A corruption of the French 'pour la gare', it originally meant station porters before coming to refer to a group of petty thieves who gathered close to the station, and is specific to Sibiu in the early twentieth century. Romanian and Saxon food words are foreign to German readers too, so I have kept them as in the original. But as Germany uses different place names, a glossary has been added.

I am grateful to Iris Wolff for her generosity and patience in answering my questions, to Monique Charlesworth for her extraordinarily perceptive editorial eye, and to Marina, Mike and everyone else who helped with terminology and images along the way.

**Ruth Martin**

# GLOSSARY OF PLACE NAMES

· · · · ·

Romania is a country of many languages. The German-speaking characters in this book refer to its towns and cities, rivers and mountains by their German names and these have been retained in the text. Below are the Romanian equivalents as they appear on the country's official maps. **RM**

**Rivers and mountains**

| *German* | *Romanian* |
| --- | --- |
| Fogarasch Mountains | Făgăraş Mountains |
| Marosch | Mureş |
| Zibin | Cibin |

**Towns and cities**

| | |
| --- | --- |
| Agnetheln | Agnita |
| Heltau | Cisnădie |
| Hermannstadt | Sibiu |
| Hohe Rinne | Păltiniş (a ski and health resort in the Carpathians) |
| Michelsberg | Cisnădioara (a village near Cisnădie) |
| Temeswar | Timişoara |

To be published by Moth Books in 2026